MW00749534

WHO LOVES ALEX BEST?

Meghan mcLeod

WHO LOVES ALEX BEST?

TRUDY MORGAN

REVIEW AND HERALD® PUBLISHING ASSOCIATION
HAGERSTOWN, MD 21740

THE BEST FRIENDS SERIES

Copyright © 1996 by
Review and Herald® Publishing Association

The author assumes full responsibility for the accuracy of all facts
and quotations as cited in this book.

This book was
Edited by Gerald Wheeler
Interior design by Patricia S. Wegh
Cover design by De Laine Heinlein-Mayden
Cover photo by Joel D. Springer
Typeset: 10/11 Times Roman

PRINTED IN U.S.A.

00 99 98 97 96   10 9 8 7 6 5 4 3 2 1

R&H Cataloging Service
Morgan, Trudy J
    Who loves Alex Best?

    I. Title.

        813.54

ISBN 0-8280-1063-3

CHAPTER

1

ome on Alex, back to work!" Lacey's cheery voice cuts into my warm, daydreamy world.

Rolling over onto my stomach, I look up at her. "I'm already at work," I explain. "Working on my tan."

Lacey flicks me with her beach towel. "Admit it, you just want to be black like me," she says with a grin. "Never gonna happen, girlfriend. Hurry up, it's five to three."

At 3:00 our suppertime shift at the camp cafeteria starts. My couple hours of sunbathing are sadly over. Although my mind knows this, I'm just not sure how to break it to my body.

Without much enthusiasm I follow Lacey up the path from the beach toward our cabin—Cabin 14. It's one of the staff cabins across from the lodge—a small white-painted box with six bunks, occupied by six girls from Prairie Vista Academy who are all on staff here at Camp Westhaven. Lacey's bunk is underneath mine. Across from mine is a tangled lump of sleeping bag that belongs to Jackie Brooks, who works on the janitorial crew. Heather, who takes care of the horses, has the other top bunk, and the other two bottom bunks, with their sleeping bags smoothed out neatly and clothes folded in a tidy pile at the foot of the bed, belong to Vanessa Andrews and Liesl Schmidt. They're both on the waterfront staff, and both really attractive, popular girls who are going into their senior year at PVA.

Liesl's cool—she's a good friend of mine, and, although she's popular and really pretty, she's not at all stuck-up. I guess you could call Vanessa a friend too, although I'd rather not call her at all if I didn't have to. She's a major snob, though she can be good for a laugh if she forgets how wonderful she is just for a millisecond or two.

Quickly slipping on shorts and a T-shirt over my swimsuit, I race up to the cafeteria where my job for the afternoon is to slice up veggies for tonight's salad. I must say that coming to camp hasn't given me much of a break from school, since I also work in the cafe at PVA. Whole days go by when I still think I'm back at the academy cafeteria.

No, that's not true. The half-door between the kitchen and outside is open and a lovely fresh breeze off the lake blows in. Even though the camp kitchen is just as hot as the school kitchen would be on an early August day, you don't feel like you're being smothered. And the best part is that when work ends for the day, I can go to the beach or horseback riding or down to the campfire. No classes or homework or tests. Yeah, camp is definitely an improvement over school.

Oh, there's one other little bonus I forgot to mention. Back at PVA my social life is as dry as the Sahara desert. Sure, I've got lots of friends, but when it comes to guys, forget it. My biggest excitement this last school year was gazing at the back of Mike McConnell's head and wondering why he had stopped talking to me. I wasn't totally ignored by the male species, though. My geeky friend Walt Rubenik thinks I'm the most gorgeous woman at PVA. Too bad for both of us. Although from what I heard when he was up here for a weekend visit, even Walt's got a girl who's interested in him now. There goes my one and only admirer at PVA.

Camp is better. Better mainly because of Dave Vickers,

who I haven't seen all day but who comes by after I've been working for a while and hangs over the half-door talking to me while I chop celery. "What kind of potion are the kitchen witches brewing up for supper tonight?" he wants to know.

"If you don't stop talking sassy to me, it'll be something that'll turn you into a frog," I threaten.

"Does that mean you'll have to kiss me to turn me back into a handsome prince?" Dave says, a big grin splitting his face. "All right!"

"Hey, none of that," Doretha, who's our supervisor, says. "Dave, don't you have some little brats you could be chasing after?" Dave's a CIT—counselor in training.

"They're all off at crafts," he says smugly. "Robbie and Paul are taking leathercraft. They asked me if I wanted them to make me a belt or a wallet, and I said they should make a leather miniskirt for Alex!"

I snap at him with a nearby dishtowel. "You better *not* have told them that!"

"What do you think I am?" Dave says. "I wouldn't go saying that kind of thing to innocent young boys."

"You're distracting me from my work. You'll have to go."

Dave ducks away from another snap of the dishtowel. "I'll be back," he promises.

Lacey smiles over at me from the stove. Lots of us kitchen girls have guys dropping by the window to talk or flirt—Lacey herself has this guy, Jared, who's madly in love with her—but I can tell they think it's cute when Dave and I are together. And I guess together is what we are.

Because he doesn't go to PVA, I'd never met him before this summer. He attends public school, where he'll be a junior next year—like me. Dave's really funny and sweet too. I know that doesn't sound like I'm head-over-heels in love or anything. Maybe I'm not. I just don't know. He's cute, with blond hair and blue eyes, is taller than I am, and has an OK body, but he's not some major stud like Mike McConnell. That's all right. Looks don't matter that much to me.

"Alex! Wake up, Alex!" Doretha's voice cuts through my

7

daydreams. "Prince Charming's gone now. Can you come back to work?"

I look down at the chopped celery on the counter. "I'm working!"

"Yeah, only I asked you twice to wash out these bowls for me and the line was busy both times."

"Sorry, I'll have to get Call Waiting for my brain," I tell her as I head over to the sink. That cracks her up. Everyone thinks I'm the big comedian of the kitchen staff. I do like it when I can make people laugh. Sometimes, though, they're laughing *at* me. Like Lacey's doing now.

"Must be love," she says under her breath as I pass by.

"It must be," I agree. But is it? I'm not sure.

At supper that night Dave winks at me as he goes through line. "Save an extra big piece of cake for me," he says.

"It's brownies tonight."

"OK, a big brownie then. Any ice cream?"

As usual, he's surrounded by loud, messy little boys. This week's camp is a special one for underprivileged kids from inner-city neighborhoods. They're even more of a pain than the regular junior campers were. But Dave says he enjoys working with kids like that. That's one of the things I like about him. He really seems to like helping people.

After supper I'm off duty in time to take a tray out to the dining hall and sit at a table where a few of my friends are still talking, dawdling over dessert. Dave and his campers have gone already, but Heather, Trevor, Bruce, and Jackie are at the table discussing about who will be up for Family Camp, which starts the day after tomorrow.

"My folks and my sister are coming up for sure," Heather says. "And Stacey's family. Is Stacey coming, Bruce?"

Bruce shrugs. All last year he was going out with Heather's best friend and roommate, Stacey. They were a really good couple, but right before the end of the year they broke up because she wanted to go to music camp instead of working here at Westhaven. If you ask me, Bruce was kind of a jerk about the whole thing, and he deserved to get dumped.

But I know for a fact he's still crazy about her. Now he just says, "Her music camp's over this week. She says she might show up for Family Camp if her folks are here."

"That would be so cool," Heather says. "I can't wait to hear all about her summer at music camp."

Turning from their conversation to Jackie, who's kind of quiet, I ask, "How's life on the scrubbing crew?"

She makes a face. "Today we were painting. There's a whole bunch of cabins that have to be painted before Family Camp. It's a change from mopping floors, anyway. Oh, I got a letter from Tammy today."

"A letter from Tammy? Wild. I didn't know she wrote letters."

"Once in a while. Sounds like she's having a wild time in Lemoine over the summer. She's living with Crystal Delacini in the apartment."

Maybe I should explain that school has a lot of different cliques. Well, I guess that's not just a PVA thing—any school is like that. Up here at camp it's not so bad. There are still some Beautiful People and some nerds, but working together over the whole summer kind of brings the staff together. Back at school, Jackie hangs out with this crowd of sort of tough kids who are usually in some kind of trouble. Their queen bee is Tammy Doneski, who was my roommate when I first arrived at PVA last summer. Now I hang around more with other people, like Stacey and Heather and my roommate, Dana. Although I've got a lot of different friends, I kind of don't feel comfortable belonging to any one certain group. It used to be my big dream to be in a clique of special friends, but my first few months at PVA turned me off that.

Anyway, up here at camp Jackie's starting to fit in a little with my other friends and turning out not to be so much of a downer as she always was last year. But she still keeps in touch with this other group back at school I guess, and they were up here a couple weekends ago visiting. I hardly saw them, except I that went for a walk with Walt Rubenik and broke the news to him that I was going out with Dave. I only talked to Tammy

9

once, but I didn't tell anyone about our conversation.

"So what did she have to say?" I ask Jackie, casually.

"Oh, the usual stuff." She starts stacking things on her tray. "You know, she goes to all these parties, she gets drunk, she makes out with different guys, she thinks she's the coolest person on earth." Tammy and her friends don't pay much attention to school rules, and since she's not at PVA this summer, I guess she's not living by any rules at all. "Just trying to impress me how tough she is and how stupid I am for working at camp. Anyway, it was all like that. Did you have a chance to talk to her any when she was up here?"

"Umm, just a little." The others are getting up from the table, leaving Jackie and me there talking. "Like you said, I think she was trying to show off a little. She's really on her own this summer, living with Crystal and doing pretty much whatever she wants."

"Well, her parents have more or less given up trying to keep track of her."

"Sometimes I wish my parents would do that."

"Yeah, but what if you turned into Tammy?" Jackie cracks a smile, which she doesn't usually. She has this permanently mad expression, even when she's actually happy. "Anyway, did you tell her about you and Dave?"

"Um, no. I told Walt, though. Why?"

Jackie shrugs. "Just something Tammy said."

"About what?"

"About Mike McConnell asking about you."

"Oh, really?"

"Yeah. She didn't say anything to you?"

"Uh, well, yeah, she did, actually. She told me Mike wanted to say hi to me. He wanted to know what I was up to."

Jackie eyes me carefully across the table. She knows I used to like Mike, that last summer we sort of went out for a couple of weeks until he dumped me. Also she thinks I'm crazy for liking a guy like Mike, who's such a stud that he flirts with every girl he sees. But she must know by now that I'm over Mike. Long ago. Coming to camp and meeting Dave has helped me work Mike out of my system. It's no big deal for Mike to say hi to me. Although we weren't talking for most of the school year, we got friendly again on the mission trip to Santa Liana. While we didn't exactly hang around together for the rest of the spring, we did talk sometimes. There's nothing important at all about Mike saying hi to me.

So how come, when Dave drops by the cabin to get me on the way to campfire that night, am I still thinking about Mike? As we walk over to the campfire bowl, Dave chatting happily about his busy day, I steal little sidelong glances at him. I never really compared him to Mike before. Mike's at least three or four inches taller, and while there's nothing wrong with Dave's body—I wouldn't call him scrawny or anything—he hasn't got the bulging muscles Mike's got. Mike works out; I know he does. And he has dark-brown hair and these deep dark eyes that look just like someone out of a movie or a romance novel. Dave just looks cute. Cute, not gorgeous. And definitely not mysterious.

"You're quiet tonight," he says as we slip into our places on the campfire benches. Dave's sitting with his unit of boys so I find a spot on the end of the bench, near them but not exactly next to them.

"Oh, you know, Friday night," I say vaguely. "Just in a peaceful mood, I guess."

Friday night is really the most peaceful night of every week at camp. As the guitarists and songleaders take their places up front, the harmony of everyone's voices mixing in song sounds better than it does on any other night. There aren't so many kids poking each other and squirming. Everyone's gearing down, getting ready for Sabbath, tired out from the week of excitement and activities. As the voices around the fire blend in a slow, mellow chorus of "He's My Lord" and the sky deepens to a twilight blue behind the towering pine trees, I let Dave slip his hand over mine. Even though I used to hate song services and sing-alongs back at academy, here I join in loud and clear. It's a whole different atmosphere from school, somehow, and I find myself welcoming Friday nights.

We have no regular staff meeting after campfire and Afterglow on Friday nights, but a few groups of staff members are getting together up in the lodge to plan some activities for Sabbath. After I say goodnight to Dave, who has to go back to the cabin with his campers, I drift on over to the lodge and find Bruce, Heather, Trevor, Jackie, Jared, and Lacey all sprawled on two corner couches.

"We're trying to get these guys to help with a skit," Heather says, with a wave of her hand to indicate that "we" is herself and Lacey and "these guys" are the boys and Jackie. "You'll help us out, won't you, Alex?"

"Maybe. What's it about?"

As Heather plunges into explaining the skit she has to do for Sabbath school, the door to the lodge swings open and Mr. and Mrs. Edwards walk in. They're greeted with a chorus of hellos; they've been gone since yesterday. Back at school he's the Bible teacher and she teaches socials, but up here they're just part of the staff, and we all get along great. I don't even think of them so much as teachers when we're up here. Of course, they were our sponsors down in Santa Liana too, so I'm pretty used to having them around.

"We picked up the mail while we were in town!" Mrs. Edwards calls. "Anyone want to come see what we got?"

Everyone races to the front of the room, eager for their mail. I usually don't get very much—the occasional note from my mom, from my roommate, Dana, or my friend Marijo back in Fairview. Nothing to be really excited about.

Sure enough, after a few minutes of sorting through envelopes and pressing them into eager hands, Mrs. Edwards passes me a small neat envelope with my mom's familiar handwriting on it. I haven't heard from her in a couple weeks. Some kids are always getting long-distance phone calls and care packages from home, but given the way I've gotten along with my parents the last couple of years, I'm happy just to receive a letter now and then.

"Another one for you, Alex," Mrs. Edwards calls out. As I reach for the envelope, Heather says, "Maybe it's from

Stacey. She wrote me a postcard."

But as soon as I take the small white envelope I know it is not one of Stacey's notes in her cute, round curly handwriting. On this envelope my name appears in a pinched scrawl, in pencil. It looks like the sort of thing only a guy would write—one guy, in particular. My heart turns over.

"Who's it from?" Lacey asks, looking over my shoulder.

"Don't know." I head back to the couch where we were all slouched a few minutes ago. As the others return with their mail, I make myself open my mother's note and skim through that first. No really new or shocking news from home. The note's short, and as I fold it up, Heather's back, reading her postcard from Stacey out loud. I turn the other envelope over in my hand. The postmark says Lemoine. And it's definitely a guy's handwriting—one I think I recognize. But there are lots of guys in Lemoine. Even Walt is there over the summer. He could easily write me. But I know Walt's handwriting, and this isn't it.

I tear open the envelope. It's one page—not even a whole page—written in pencil on loose-leaf.

"Hi Alex,

"Bet you never expected to hear from me. I'm not much of a letter writer ha ha. But I been thinking about you a lot lately. Tammy said she saw you when she went up to camp for the weekend. I'm stuck back here in Lemoine working in the woodwork shop again. But at least I'm not living on campus so I can have a little fun, if you know what I mean. I'd really like to see you again. My dad and stepmother and the boys are going up for family camp so I might pop up for a day or two. I've been thinking a lot about last summer and all the good times we had together. Anyway I better go. Take care of yourself.

Love,
Mike"

13

As I turn the paper over and over in my hands, my heart thuds in my chest. My hands are even shaking a little. Somewhere in the background I can hear Heather and Lacey still discussing the skit for tomorrow. I think one of them has just asked me something, but I have no idea what. "Yeah, OK, whatever," I respond absentmindedly.

Pastor Howell, the camp director, is quieting everyone down, organizing all the little groups of staffers in the lounge, making some announcements about Sabbath school and church tomorrow. "OK, since so many of you are together now, let's close off the evening with a prayer, and then let's start heading back to the cabins."

As everyone bows his or her head, my mind whirls. This last year I've stopped just tuning out whenever someone's praying up front. In fact, I've really started trying to talk to God for myself, but right now I've no idea what to say to Him. I can't pray for God to get me and Mike back together, can I? Is that really what I want? I'm not sure. But right now, I feel like I want to be with Mike McConnell more than anything else on earth.

I trail along behind my friends as we leave the lodge and head over to the cabins. "Come up to the bathroom with me, Alex," Jackie says.

I turn right on the path behind her. We pass a noisy group of little boys returning from the washroom and shower block with a counselor, their flashlights bobbing in the darkness. As they get within the circle of our own flashlights, I see that the counselor is Dave.

"Hi, Alex," Dave says, slowing down for a minute.

"Hi, Dave." I can't think of anything else to say.

"See you at breakfast," he says.

"I'm working breakfast," I say.

"Well, then I'll see you in Sabbath school, OK?"

"OK." We can't kiss each other goodnight or anything, not with all the kids around, so he gives me a quick squeeze on the shoulder and then walks on.

Now I'm more confused than ever. Dave's smile is so

sweet and warm. I know he really cares about me. Even when I was going out with Mike, I didn't feel like he cared about me the way Dave does. But he was more exciting. And getting a letter from him after all these months of silence is definitely exciting.

By the time I'm back in my bunk with my sleeping bag pulled up over my ears, I still haven't straightened out how I feel. It's a relief to be able to go to sleep.

CHAPTER

2

Y ou sure nothing's wrong?" Dave asks for about the millionth time.

"I'm sure," I say. Even I recognize that I don't sound very welcoming.

"Because if there's anything bothering you— Hey, Gary! Get back here! Leave that alone!" He tears off after one of the campers who's throwing rocks at a bird's nest. We're taking a hike through the beautiful state park about 20 miles from Camp Westhaven. Some of these inner-city kids have never been out of the city and have never seen places like this. The trail winds through miles of woods, with beautiful lakes and hills. Since I got up at 4:00 a.m. to work the breakfast shift in the cafeteria, then went to Sabbath school and church service and worked through lunch, I wasn't going to come on the hike this afternoon. I had planned to crash in my bunk and catch up on my sleep. But Dave talked me into coming. Bet he's sorry now he did that. I haven't been the world's greatest company for him.

Since he's busy with the kids, I fall into step beside

Heather. "You must be wasted," she says. "You were up so early this morning."

"Yeah, I'm tired. I should've stayed back and slept. That's what Jackie's doing."

"And she wasn't even up that early. Well, today's the last day of this camp. Next week'll be a lot different," Heather says.

"You must be looking forward to seeing your folks."

"Yeah, I am," she admits. "What about Dave? Are his folks coming up? You haven't met them yet, have you?"

"Um—no, I don't think they're coming. No, I haven't met them."

"Has he met your folks?"

"No." I roll my eyes. Heather, like most of my friends, has some clue that my parents aren't exactly 100 percent supportive of everything I do, but she doesn't really know how crazy they can get. Last summer my dad practically freaked out about me dating Mike. I don't know what's going to happen when they find out about Dave.

"So tell me honestly now," Heather says, obviously settling in for a real girl talk, "how serious is this? You and Dave. Is it just a summertime thing, or do you think you'll keep in touch when you get back to PVA?"

"Oh, Heather, I haven't got a clue!" Suddenly I feel like being a lot more honest than I'd planned on. "Can you keep a secret?"

"Sure, of course."

"Well, I'm really mixed up about Dave. I mean, there's nothing wrong with him, he's great. It's just—another guy."

Heather's blue eyes widen. "Another guy? Someone up here?" I can see her brain ticking over, running through all the guys on the camp staff, wondering which one I could be interested in.

"No, not up here. Someone back at PVA. I haven't thought much about him in a long time, but I got a letter from him yesterday. It looks like he's still thinking about me."

Heather glances around, lowers her voice, draws her head close to mine. "It's not—Walt, is it?"

"*Heather!*" For a moment my mood lifts, and I almost want to laugh. I give her a poke in the shoulder, sending her stumbling to the edge of the path. "Get real! Do you think I'd be thinking of dropping a cool guy like Dave for *Walt Rubenik?* Besides, I think Walt's actually interested in someone else now, thank goodness! No, this is someone else."

"Someone I know?"

"Um, yeah, I guess." That's stupid. Everyone at PVA knows everyone else to some degree, and everyone definitely knows Mike McConnell. He's one of the most popular guys on campus. "But not someone you know real well. I mean, not someone we usually hang out with or anything."

"It's—it's not Mike McConnell, is it?"

Wow! How'd she *do* that? I mean, I thought I'd been pretty subtle about liking Mike. It's true, I used to date him for about 15 seconds last summer, but Heather didn't know me then, so how could she know about Mike? I wonder if I've been a lot more obvious than I thought. Maybe without realizing it I've been walking around PVA all year wearing a huge neon sign on my back that says, "I'm in love with Mike McConnell!"

"Well, yeah—yeah, it is Mike. See, I went out with him last summer."

"I know, I heard about that."

Sorry, I guess I *haven't* been wearing a neon sign. I just forgot for a moment that the PVA campus is the most gossippy place on earth. Everyone knows everyone's business, and I guess that includes about me and Mike. But then, there aren't many girls who haven't had a crush on Mike at sometime or another.

"Anyway," Heather goes on, just as if I'd asked her advice or something, "I think you're better off with Dave. He's a lot nicer than Mike is."

I can think of about 30 million sarcastic things to say, but I manage to keep my mouth shut for a few seconds. Then I say, "Well, he probably is, but Mike's better looking."

"Looks aren't everything," Heather persists.

This time I *really* want to make a smart-mouthed remark,

like how she must believe that or she wouldn't be going out with Trevor, who is no studmuffin, let me tell you, but I have to bite my tongue on that one or my friendship with her is down the tubes forever. But honestly, where does she get off telling me who I should like?

"I *know* looks aren't everything!" We pause at a little lookout with a fence rail running along by a brook and Heather leans against the rail to gaze down into the brook. I stand there too, staring down into the water and trying to pull my thoughts together. "It's not just looks. I really liked Mike a lot, and when he dumped me, it took a long time to get over it. If he's interested again now—well, I'd just like to know. I can't forget about him that easily."

A chorus of yelling on the path behind us clears the way for another group of little kids. It's Dave and his boys, along with their senior counselor, a college guy called Randy. Dave rolls his eyes and grins at me as they pass.

"But Dave's so *sweet*," Heather says when they're out of earshot.

"I know he is!" Picking up a handful of pebbles, I plunk them one by one into the stream. *Sweet* is just the word I use to describe Dave in my head. Problem is, I'm not sure *sweet* is exactly what I'm looking for in a guy. "Don't get me wrong—I still like Dave a lot. I don't want to hurt him. I've just been thinking a lot about Mike lately."

Heather nods. "Yeah, well, once you've liked somebody it's hard to get them out of your system sometimes. I remember Paul, this guy I liked before Trevor . . . "

She goes on happily with her own story, and we head back on the trail with the others as Heather chatters away. I'm still trying to work things out in my own mind, but all it's giving me is a headache.

After the hike we climb back onto the buses waiting in the parking lot. At the back of the bus I can see Dave saving an empty seat beside him and waving to me frantically. I slide in next to him. The sun-warmed vinyl seat feels good on my bare legs, and I feel good inside, too, knowing this nice guy cares enough to save me a seat and look so happy that I'm here with him. Even when I've been such a grouch all day. I really don't deserve someone this nice. I tell myself sternly that I'm crazy to be even thinking about a jerk like Mike McConnell.

Back at the camp, I'm able to relax over supper since I'm not on supper duty, though I do have to go in for a couple of hours afterward to help clean up. Then we're all free for the evening program.

The Saturday night program is always a highlight of camp. First we have campfire worship, and then after sunset different cabins and groups put on skits and do songs and stuff. There's usually a marshmallow roast, and finally some big group game like Capture the Flag or a team waterfight, just to get the campers exhausted so they'll sleep instead of running around pulling pranks all night.

This Saturday night is no exception. Some of the kitchen crew are up front doing a song, which I join in with despite the fact that I have absolutely no singing talent at all. I'm amazed by the stuff I'll get up front and do now, at least if there's a crowd up there with me—things I would never have dreamed of a year ago before I came to PVA. Working at camp has really made me a lot less nervous about stuff. Then some of the kids and their counselors take the stage. Dave and Randy's unit does a skit that has everyone cracking up laughing. When it's over, Dave sits next to me—Randy must have told him he could take a break from watching the kids.

"That was great," I tell him as he slides onto the wooden bench beside me. "It was really funny."

"You were pretty good up there yourself," he says, and once again he squeezes my hand. I wish I felt shivers going down my spine when he does that, but all I feel is comfortable and warm and safe. Still, I hope we can get a few minutes alone later in the evening. That's not very easy to find up here at camp.

But we do manage—even though it's only about 10 minutes when the game of Capture the Flag is over and the tired campers are heading down to the cafeteria for juice and cookies. Dave catches up with me as I'm walking back toward the lodge alone, grabs hold of my hand, and leads me a little ways off the path toward the stables.

"How are you doing, Alex?" he asks softly when we're alone in the moonlight. Voices and laughter filter up through the trees, but no one can see us.

"I'm pretty good," I tell him. "It's been a good day."

"Got to get up early again tomorrow?"

"Four o'clock once again. It doesn't matter, I'm used to it."

He leans forward and kisses me very gently. The first time Dave kissed me was only about two weeks ago, after we'd been hanging around together nearly all summer. That was weird—totally unlike the way it was with Mike. With Mike, almost the first thing he did was kiss me—before we even really knew each other. It was very exciting. By the time Dave kissed me I felt like I knew him so well he was almost like one of my friends or something. Don't get me wrong now—he's a good kisser, but it just wasn't quite as thrilling as that time with Mike.

Of course, Dave has no idea what I'm thinking, but he can tell my mind's somewhere else. "We'd better get back," he says, taking hold of my hand firmly and heading toward the main path.

That's another thing different about last summer with Mike and this summer with Dave. Rules about making out and stuff are pretty strict at PVA, but you can get away with a lot if you know the right places to go at the right times, and Mike always did. I guess he had experience. Most of the time we spent together was kissing and stuff at the back of the gymnasium. And Mike really didn't care about breaking rules. I didn't either, back then. Either of us would do whatever we could get away with.

This summer is totally different. Up at camp we have the same rules as at school, but when you're a staff member you have to set a good example and everything, so it's even harder to get away with stuff. Especially since we're so busy all the time. So most of the time I've spent with Dave has been doing things with other people around, like canoeing or horseback riding or just hanging out at mealtimes and stuff. Not many quiet romantic evenings alone. And I don't really want to mess things up this summer, being on staff and everything, and Dave's even more careful than I am. I mean, it's not like he doesn't want to get alone with me, but he's basically a good guy who likes to follow the rules and stay out of trouble. Total opposite of Mike.

". . . and anyway, I was thinking that we could— Alex? Are you listening?"

"Huh? Oh, sorry." We're walking up to the lodge, and Dave is obviously in the middle of saying something, but I have no idea what it is. I can't even fake it. "Sorry, I was thinking about something."

"Like you've been doing all day," Dave says, and I can hear the edge of impatience in his voice. "Listen, Alex, if anything's wrong I really wish you'd tell me."

But I don't. How can I tell him about Mike? I do care about Dave. After all, I don't want to lose him—especially when there's no guarantee I'll be getting Mike back. This is such a mess. I fall into bed that night hoping the whole problem will just disappear.

For a while the next day it seems like it has. Once again I roll out of my bunk early and get to work making and serving breakfast in the kitchen. I only see Dave for a second, as he's coming through line, and he looks friendly, like he normally does. The rest of the morning is a blur of busyness. The campers leave in buses and cars for the trip home, and the staff all get busy preparing for family camp. People will start arriving this evening.

Family camp is a break for the counselors, since all the kids are staying with parents and grandparents or whatever. But there are a lot more activities planned to keep everyone busy—sports and crafts and stuff—so all the counselors and CITs are doing other jobs. For those of us in the kitchen, things stay pretty much the same. I spend most of the afternoon peeling potatoes for potato salad at supper. People keep rushing in and out with news of whose family has arrived and whose friends are coming.

When I finally get my break at about 3:00 in the afternoon, I'm eager to head down to the water for a swim. There's no one in the cabin when I change into my swimsuit and grab a towel, but some staff members are splashing around down by the dock, taking advantage of a few free minutes. Josh, the good-looking waterskiing instructor, is just back in from skiing and calls out to ask if anyone else wants a turn. I've actually learned to ski this summer—I'm not great, but I can get around—but I don't want to do anything that challenging now. Just lie on my back in the water and enjoy the hot, hot sun streaming down.

As I'm wading back in toward the beach, I see Dave with a couple of other guys head toward the dock. I wave to him, but instead of coming over he just nods and walks on.

Now that's weird. Dave never, and I mean never, acts like that. I get out of the water and follow him down to the dock, but he keeps his back to me until I tap him on the shoulder. When he turns to me, he's frowning, and I don't think it's just that he's got the sun in his eyes.

"What's up?" I ask.

"Not much," he says. "Just going to do some skiing if I can find a few minutes."

"You wouldn't like to take a canoe out, would you?"

He frowns even deeper. "No thanks, I want to go skiing."

Suddenly I really want to make him snap out of this mood. "Aw, come on. You can go skiing later."

"No, Alex!" he almost snaps at me. "I've only got half an hour free, and I want to go skiing, OK?"

"Sure, whatever," I say, backing away. Wonder what's wrong with him?

It's only then that I notice that one of the guys he's with is Heather's boyfriend, Trevor, and Trevor, who's usually a pretty good friend of mine, is also avoiding looking at me. Suddenly I start putting two and two together and coming up with a number I don't like very much.

Turning away from the dock without even saying goodbye to Dave—not like he's saying goodbye to me either—I stomp up from the beach toward Cabin 14. Stripping off my dripping wet suit and toweling my body briskly, I think of all the things I'd like to say to Heather. But she catches me off guard, coming in just as I'm pulling my T-shirt over my head.

I guess my red-haired temper takes over, because as soon as she says, "Hi, Alex," I demand, "Did you tell Dave what I was saying yesterday about Mike?"

She looks guilty. "No—no, of course not."

"Did you tell *anyone?* Like maybe Trevor?"

Heather looks away. "Well, yeah, I did tell Trevor. Not the whole thing," she adds quickly. "Just—well, he was saying Dave was upset last night because you seemed to be cutting him off or something, you were acting weird, so I told Trevor there was another guy you used to like and you'd just heard from him. I didn't tell Trevor who it was," she adds in a voice that doesn't totally convince me. Like maybe she didn't tell him, but she let him guess or something.

"Great! Thanks a million, Heather, you've made my life so much easier! He's gone and told Dave!"

"Oh, I don't think he did that—"

"Yeah? Well, then why did I just see Dave down at the docks, and he treated me like I had leprosy or something?"

"Well, maybe it's just because of the way you were acting yesterday."

I stop to think about this for a second. "No way. I saw him at breakfast, and he wasn't rude to me then. And I haven't seen him since. Something's happened since this morning to make him mad at me—and it's *your* fault!"

"It's your own fault!" Heather shoots back. "If you're going out with one guy and dreaming about another, don't blame me if you can't make up your mind!"

"I was going to make up my mind!" I yell. "I just wanted a little time to do it without my private business being broadcast all over Camp Westhaven!" With that I slam the door behind me.

Outside the sun is still shining, birds are still singing, and a light breeze stirs the tops of the trees, but I feel like I'm carrying black storm clouds around with me. Heading across the campgrounds, oblivious to everything around me, I almost bump right into Dave, of all people, returning from the beach.

"Sorry," he says, starting to walk away.

"Dave! Wait!"

"What?"

"Come for a walk with me or something?"

He rolls his eyes. "Alex, I told you I only had a short break. I've got to get back to work. We're clearing out some brush from one of the campsites."

"Oh, come on. Be a little late. I want to—to talk to you." Actually I'm not sure talking to Dave is exactly what I want to do, but I want to be with him. I want to make everything all right.

Dave glances at his watch, then at me. "OK, but only for a couple of minutes. Then I really have to get back to work."

I fall into step beside him as we take the trail toward the stables. Although I'd like to ignore the whole problem, just talk about other stuff, suddenly it seems as if we have nothing else to speak about. Dave and I have always found it real easy to talk. Now he's not talking and I'm not either. My throat has a lump the size of an orange.

"Listen, Dave," I blurt out suddenly, "did Heather or Trevor tell you something about me? About something I said?"

He looks at me with a funny expression, and I can't quite figure out what it is. I think he's angry, but it also looks like he's almost pleased with me for coming right out and saying it. He doesn't say anything for a minute, then he says, "Yeah, Trevor said something."

"Heather was shooting off her mouth when she had no right to. I just told her something I was thinking about, and she went and told Trevor. I never meant to say any of that."

"Yeah, but—that doesn't change anything, does it? I mean, it's still true."

I kick a little pebble that's appeared in the path at my feet. "Well—I don't know. What did Trevor tell you?"

"That the reason you were acting weird is there's this other guy you like, back at PVA, and you got a letter from him."

I nod. Not much to argue with there. "Yeah, that's true, but Dave—you're reading too much into it. I mean, yeah, I got a letter from this guy, and I wondered why because we hadn't spoken for a long time. I did used to like him. But not anymore. I haven't liked him for ages. I was just—confused about the letter. It's not like I don't want to see you anymore or anything. I like you much better than him." There. How's that for being straightforward and blunt?

Dave lets out a big sigh. After a minute he says, "Well, I can see how you would feel kind of confused if a guy you used to like suddenly wrote you right out of the blue."

That's the great thing about Dave—he's so understanding, and he hardly ever gets mad. "But I'm telling you the truth, Dave; he doesn't mean anything to me anymore." Dave and I are not the types to fall all over each other saying I love you and stuff—it hasn't been like that with us—but I hope he gets the message.

It seems like he does. He gives me a hug. "Well, I'm glad he doesn't," he says, and as we head back to the cabins he's got his usual big grin again. When he leaves for work, I feel much better.

There's only two things still wrong, I remember, as my sad feeling sweeps back over me again. First, there's my so-called friend Heather and what she did to me. And second, there's the fact that I really don't know if the stuff I told Dave is the truth or not.

CHAPTER

3

Now it's 8:00 on Sunday night, and after the day's busyness things have quieted down for the staff. No campfire tonight—everyone is still arriving and getting registered for Family Camp. Families pour into the lodge, signing up for cabins or campsites and getting meal tickets. Some of us staffers whose work is done for the day sit around on the couches, saying hi to people we know and discussing plans for the week.

Dave and I are with Jackie and her friend Jared—the guy who's got such a crush on Lacey. But Lacey's avoiding him; she's way over on the other side of the room with Heather, Trevor, and Bruce. The separation between the two groups isn't just because of Lacey and Jared. It's me and Heather too. Since this afternoon when I found out that she'd told Dave what I said about Mike, I've been so mad I can't even stand the thought of seeing her. The only time I had to come face to face with her was in the cafeteria line at supper—I was working behind the counter—and we just avoided looking at each other.

Just then the door to the lodge opens as another family enters, trailing sleeping bags and suitcases. From the other side of the lodge there's a happy shriek and Heather jumps up from her seat and flies toward the door. Then I see who it is that's just arrived—Stacey, Heather's roommate at school, who's been at music camp all summer.

Stacey squeals too and the two of them shoot across the room and wrap each other in a huge hug. Lacey and Trevor run over too, and Bruce walks behind them kind of slowly, as if he's not quite sure how happy this meeting between him and Stacey is going to be. From my perch on the corner couch, I watch with interest, listening with one ear as Jackie explains to Dave and Jared, who don't know the PVA crowd, who Stacey is.

Of course Stacey's a friend of mine as well. Around the end of last year, she and Heather and my roommate, Dana, were just about my best friends. Normally I'd be over there all wild and hugging her too. But the whole Heather thing is going to make this difficult.

Anyway, I wouldn't want to interrupt right now, because Stacey's saying hi to Bruce. They both look a little nervous, then she steps forward, and he gives her a hug. It's hard to tell exactly what kind of a hug it is—romantic or not romantic. I have a feeling Bruce still wants to get back together with her, but you never know for sure. This should be an interesting week.

Then Stacey, glancing around the room, spots me, and I jump up off the couch and go over to say hi. We're all standing around in this big happy group, listening to her tell about music camp and the big musical at the end of it that she got to have a part in, and yet every time I catch Heather's eye, I feel like we're in the arctic and somebody just opened the door and let in a blast of freezing air. Well, I'm sure the looks I'm giving her are not that nice either.

Stacey doesn't seem to notice the awkwardness, but a few minutes later when she goes off with her parents and her two little brothers to get settled, I peel away from Heather's gang and head back to Dave and my other friends on the couch.

"You'll have to meet Stacey later," I tell Dave. "She's cool." I feel as if I should have dragged him over right away and introduced him to Stacey as my new boyfriend. A couple of days ago that's exactly what I would have done. But something's changed, and I'd be lying to pretend it hasn't.

Going back to the cabin that night is pretty uncomfortable. Usually we all talk for a while before the lights go out. Our gang in Cabin 14 is a pretty different group, with Jackie who thinks of herself as so tough and such a loser, even though she's not; and Liesl and Vanessa who are so popular and well-off and everything; with me, Lacey, and Heather as sort of the ordinary girls in the middle. But over the summer we've gotten pretty used to each other. Jackie gets grouchy sometimes, but not so much as she used to, and Vanessa goes into her big "I'm so wonderful" act, but we don't take her seriously anymore, and the six of us usually have a few good laughs together.

Not tonight. Liesl and Vanessa gab away about people who are up for the week. Jackie's quiet with her nose buried in a romance novel, a reading taste she picked up from me and her roommate Shantelle, although I don't read them as much as I used to. Heather and I are totally silent, and Lacey, who's really good friends with both of us, has also got her nose in a book as if she's desperately hoping she won't be asked to talk.

It's very awkward to have to go to bed at night in the same room with someone you're really mad at, and even more weird if you're surrounded by other people so you can't really talk it out. I'm not sure at this point that I want to speak to Heather, though. I feel like I have a pretty good right to be mad at her—after all, she did tell a secret of mine—and if anyone should make the first move toward patching things up, it should be her.

Monday morning, for the first time in days, I'm not working the breakfast shift so I have the incredible luxury of sleeping in. I stay in the bunk until 8:00. By the time I finally pry my eyelids open, everyone else has left the cabin. The breakfast line closes at 8:00, but that doesn't matter to me because

I pull on a pair of jean cutoffs and a T-shirt and go up to the kitchen, where my fellow cafeteria workers let me in, and I cut myself a big slice of the coffee cake served for breakfast. Working in the kitchen definitely has a few advantages.

After breakfast I have a couple of hours free before I start work at 10:30. I head up to the washrooms for a quick shower, and as I'm coming out I meet Stacey.

"Hi, Alex! Wow, I hardly got a chance to talk to you at all last night, what with everyone around. You busy?"

"No, I've got a little bit of free time."

"Cool. Hey, let's go up to the stables and see if we can take a couple of horses out. Maybe Heather'll have a few minutes free to come with us."

"Uh, yeah. You know, I don't feel that much like horseback riding. I was hoping to find someone who wanted to go canoeing."

"Oh, OK! Let's do that instead." Her eyes sparkle a little, and she adds, "If we go down to the waterfront I'll get to see Bruce again."

"And is that a big deal—seeing Bruce again?" I fall into step beside her. Although I haven't thought much about Stacey all summer, we were getting to be really good friends before school ended, and now that she's here I realize how much I've missed her bouncy personality.

"I *honestly* don't know," she says, rolling her eyes. "I mean, I don't know if I want to get back with him or not. After everything I went through with him last spring. But whether we do or not, it still feels good to be around him again."

I nod agreement. That's almost exactly what I'm feeling about Mike McConnell. I don't know if I really want to go out with him again, but I'd sure like to see him once more.

Things are busy down at the waterfront. There's a swimming class going on for some very little kids, some teenagers are swimming out in the deeper water, Josh is giving waterskiing lessons, and some of the canoes are out on the lake. Bruce is sitting in the lifeguard's chair in front of the boathouse.

"Hi, Bruce! Can we take a canoe out?" Stacey asks,

swinging herself up onto the base of the lifeguard's chair and looking up into his face. I really don't know if she's trying to act extra cute or if it comes naturally, but if she weren't my friend it would make me slightly ill.

Bruce, typical guy, laps it right up. He gives her this big grin and says, "Sure! Wish I didn't have to work, I'd come out with you."

"Maybe later," Stacey says, and I swear she actually bats her eyelashes at him.

"Come on, Madonna," I say, hauling at her sleeve. "Save the flirting for later."

Out on the water, slicing through the clear waters of the lake with my paddle, I answer Stacey's questions about what camp's been like all summer. Of course I tell her about me and Dave. I don't mention anything about the confusion of the past couple of days. Then I listen to her rave on about how wonderful music camp was, how exciting it felt to be singing up on stage in front of a big audience. "I've always *known* I wanted to be a singer," she says, "but after this summer I'm totally sure. It was the greatest experience ever."

"See? I told you you should go," I remind her. "I just wish . . ."

"Wish what?"

"Wish there was something for me that was as exciting as singing is for you. I mean, not like I want my whole life planned out right now or anything, but I'd like to have something that was as big for me as music is for you."

"Some people just don't make up their minds that fast," Stacey says.

"I know. But really, the only clue I've got about anything is that I love to travel. I love being someplace I've never been and learning how to fit in. I think I'm kind of good at that. But in what kind of job would I be moving somewhere new all the time?"

"Door-to-door salesman," Stacey suggests. "You could sell vacuum cleaners."

"Oh, thanks a *lot*," I say, splashing water from my paddle

31

onto the back of her head. "Yeah, I can just see me doing that. Or maybe encyclopedias."

"Or you could be an Avon lady."

"My future's really looking bright!"

Suddenly a loud roar cuts through our conversation and a speedboat swings toward us, honking its horn. For a minute I'm terrified till I look up and see that the driver is Mr. Marsh, with this crazy grin on his face. I swear, sometimes that man acts so insane its hard to remember he's a teacher. Both he and Mr. Edwards. They're just like a couple of high school guys when they get together and start fooling around. I'm not surprised to see that the other person in the boat *is* Mr. Edwards. They've obviously decided to cut as close to the canoe as they can to give us a wild ride.

As our canoe dips and dives in the wake of the speedboat, Stacey shakes her paddle threateningly at the two teachers. "We'll get you for that!" she shouts after the disappearing boat.

"Yeah, what're we going to do—cut down the speedboat with the canoe when they're not looking?"

Stacey laughs. "Hey," she says suddenly, "seeing Mr. Marsh just reminded me. Know what other PVA teacher is up here this week?"

"No, but say it's not Mr. Stevens!" Mr. Stevens is the math teacher at PVA. About 50 years old, he's a real grouch—everybody says so, even the kids who actually like math, which I'll admit I don't.

"No, someone a little nicer than that! Mrs. Krause!"

"Oh, really? Cool," I say. I never gave Mrs. Krause much thought all year. Because she's the music teacher and choir director, I've never had much to do with her, for reasons you would understand if you ever heard me sing in the shower. But after I started hanging around with Stacey—who of course takes voice lessons, is in choir, and works in the music department—I started hearing more about Mrs. Krause. She's like Stacey's absolute hero. It was her idea for Stacey to go to this music camp, and she really encouraged her a lot. She's another one of the younger faculty, like Mr. Marsh and the Edwards, and she's really pretty cool.

"I guess you'll be pretty glad to see her again and tell her about music camp," I say.

"Oh, yeah, I've got loads of stuff to tell her," Stacey says.

"Why's she up for Family Camp?" I ask. "It's not like she's got kids or anything." It does seem a bit weird because Mrs. Krause actually doesn't have a family at all. The story I heard is that her husband left her when they'd only been married a few years. It's pretty sad.

"I don't know. She came up with her parents and a friend of hers. Apparently it's a tradition; they come all the time. But I was thinking . . ."

"Thinking what?"

"Well, you know how at the end of last year we were saying how cute it would be if Mr. Marsh and Mrs. Krause got together?"

"*You* were saying. I don't believe in matchmaking, especially with teachers!"

"No, but really, Alex. Think about it. I bet they're both lonely, and they're not getting any younger. Mr. Marsh must be about 30! It's time they got together, and I think they're just perfect for each other. Wouldn't it be cool if we could— I don't know—somehow set them up?"

"Oh, yeah, and how're you supposed to do that?"

"I have no idea, but trust me, I'll think of something. They're already friends. I bet all it would take is the right moment—the right setting—and they'd fall madly in love."

I can't help laughing. Stacey's such a total romantic. But it could be fun to try to play matchmaker. At the very least, maybe we could embarrass them.

"I know!" Stacey says suddenly. We're turning the canoe around now, heading it back in toward the dock when she has her bright idea. "We could do something with couples—you know, me and Bruce, Heather and Trevor, you and Dave—something that would need a chaperone. Like go somewhere or something. And we could ask them to be our chaperones. Something romantic . . . "

"Um, maybe you're forgetting the rest of us are staff here, Stace? Like we can't just go taking off on some romantic rendezvous."

"Oh, give me a break! I just had the idea, now I've got to work out the details, OK?"

I laugh along with her, but a sick feeling takes up residence in the pit of my stomach. Of course she'll be assuming we'll all be doing stuff together again, as a gang of friends. Obviously Heather hasn't told her we're not on the best of terms. But then, what's Heather supposed to say? "Alex isn't talking to me because I told her secrets behind her back"? Heather's got her reasons for keeping her mouth shut.

Too bad she didn't start a little sooner.

By the time we reach the dock with the canoe I need to leave for work. And work keeps me busy all through the rest of the afternoon. Not until just before campfire do I have time to stop by the cabin, and when I get there, guess who's there? That's right. Heather. All by herself.

I head straight for my bunk and drag out my gym bag, pulling out my jeans and a sweatshirt in case it gets cooler later on.

"How's it going, Alex?" Heather says. Just like nothing ever happened! But I can tell from her voice that she's trying to act cool and not really pulling it off.

For a minute I consider not saying anything. It still makes me mad that she could act that way. If it hadn't been for seeing Stacey this morning, I probably wouldn't say anything. But I do remember what our gang was like at the end of last year and how good it felt to have a crowd of close girlfriends like that. Heather was part of that. She was my friend, and I guess she still is.

But I can't pretend nothing happened. "Not bad, I guess," I say, with my back still to her as I rummage through my bag for two socks that match.

"Listen, I'm really sorry," Heather blurts out. "You're still mad at me, aren't you?"

"Yeah, I guess so." Finally I turn to face her and sit down on the bunk. "Look, Heather, you had no right to go talking behind my back. You probably thought you were making things better for Dave, but you weren't. It almost messed things up totally between us. And I really still do like him. More than Mike or anyone else, OK?"

"OK." Heather looks away. "It's just—I like Dave. He's nice. I didn't want to see him hurt."

"I wasn't going to hurt him. I was just thinking things through. Out loud. Anyway, it's over now, and Dave and I have worked things out. Let's forget about it."

"OK," Heather says with what I can tell is a huge sigh of relief. "I really am sorry."

"No problem." She waits for me to finish changing, and we head down to campfire together.

I'm relieved that that's all over. As I settle down on the bench next to my friends, I think about Mike's letter and all the trouble that one little piece of paper caused. Trouble that didn't really have to happen, because Mike McConnell is definitely *not* that important to me. Like I said, I'm just glad it's all over now.

CHAPTER

4

Got the plan all worked out," Stacey announces.

"Wh-what?" I'm not at my brightest around 7:30 in the morning, especially when I've been working in the kitchen since 6:00. Ladling scoops of oatmeal into people's bowls, trying to make sure everyone gets a few raisins so they don't complain, I don't even really register that Stacey's the next person in line until she leans over the counter and says this thing about her "plan."

I'm still going "Plan? What plan?" in my head long after Stacey and her entire family have gone through line and on into the dining hall. Then I have this dim memory that yesterday, when Stacey and I were canoeing, she had some idea about trying to set up Mr. Marsh and Mrs. Krause with each other. I'm guessing that's the plan she's talking about. But who knows? The last plan Stacey and I got together on involved kidnapping plastic flamingos—though I'll have to admit that one was mostly my idea. That involved playing tricks on our teachers too, come to think of it—they were the Edwards' flamingos. But while most people don't mind a little messing around with their lawn decorations, they tend to be a little more sensitive about their love lives. I'm really not sure we should get ourselves mixed up in the Mr. Marsh/Mrs. Krause thing.

When the breakfast dishes are done, I have a couple hours off before I return in the afternoon to prepare for supper. The campgrounds are busy with new kids and their families. I head up to the stables and lean on the fence, watching Heather as she gives some tiny little kids a riding lesson. It's a cloudy day, a little cooler than most of the lovely days we've had at camp this summer. It feels like it might rain. But I'm really not in the mood for horseback riding, even if there were any horses available. I'm not sure what I feel like doing.

Since the counselors and CIT's aren't working as counselors this week, Dave has a new job. He's teaching string art, of all things. My least favorite craft when I went to camp. By the time I got my strings untangled, straightened, and sorted out, I'd spend two minutes on the actual pattern before class would be over. After leaving all my strings neat and tidy, I'd return the next day to find them all tied in a big tangled knot. As if somebody would come in at night and mess them up on purpose.

Grinning at my memories, I stick my hands deep in the pockets of my jean cutoffs and head across the campgrounds to the craft cabins. There's this whole little semicircle of cute one-room cabins up beyond the ballfield. Kids are milling around most of them, but a few cabins have adults doing crafts too. Dave, though, is teaching string art to a mixed bunch: some kids, some parents, and a couple who look old enough to be someone's grandma and grandpa.

His face brightens when he sees me. I guess he's finally gotten over our little misunderstanding. That's one of many cool things about Dave—he really doesn't hold a grudge long at all.

"Hey," I say, standing next to him, "can I learn string art?"

"Why, you like this kind of thing?" Dave asks.

"Like it? I *hate* it!" Laughing, I tell him about my previous string art experiences. "In fact," I finish, "there really aren't *any* crafts I'm good at. Do you know anyone who can mess up *plastercraft?* Painting designs on little plaques? I tried to do the 'Kitchen Prayer'—you know, the one that goes 'God bless my little kitchen Lord, I love its every nook . . .'? —and I brought it home to my mom."

"Yeah. Did she like it?"

"She *loved* it. I mean, she did the mom thing, she went on and on about it and how beautiful it was, but I found out later she had *no* idea what it said. She couldn't read any of the words. It was like 'Blob blob my little blob blob, I blob its blob blob blob . . .'"

By this time I've got Dave laughing so hard he's getting all his strings tangled up. "I don't think I can teach you string art, Alex! Maybe you should start with something easy, like this . . ." He grabs one of the boards covered in black cloth, drives a single nail into it, and wraps a single piece of colored thread around the nail. "See what you can do with that!"

Both of us are giggling so much Dave doesn't hear at first when one of the kids working on a project calls out to him. "Hey, Dave! Dave! Can you give me a hand over here?"

"Sorry, I'll be right there," Dave replies. He hurries over to where the kid, a freckle-faced boy of about 11, is making a huge mess with his string art project. "Do I hafta do string art? I'm sick of it. I wanna go do archery."

"Hey, you signed up for it," Dave says. "Don't worry, it'll be cool when you get it done. All you gotta do is . . ." He leans over, explaining patiently. For a second it flashes into my mind that he'd make a great dad. Then I can't believe I just had that thought and wipe it out of my mind instantly.

"And, there you go," Dave says, finishing up with the kid. "Just a couple more days and you'll have a string art master-piece, an original by Mr.— sorry, I forgot your name. Andy, isn't it?"

"Andy McConnell," the kid says.

"McConnell?" I realize it's me who's spoken.

The kid looks up at me, frowning. I notice a resemblance

there. He's kind of cute for an 11-year-old. "Yeah," he says.

"Are you from Wilcox?"

"Near there, yeah."

"Do you have a brother named Mike?"

"Yeah, Mike's my brother," the kid answers.

Somehow I had myself convinced that the whole Mike thing was all in the past, but as soon as Andy says that Mike's his brother, I know I've been kidding myself. The bottom of my stomach drops like an elevator cut loose from its cable, and lands somewhere around my feet. For a second I can't say anything. "Your whole family up here this week?" I manage to ask the kid, trying to sound cool like I'm just oh so casually interested. My mind is racing—does Dave know that Mike's the guy I used to like at PVA? Used to? Who am I kidding?

Andy nods. He's already lost interest in me and is squinting back down at his string art. "Yeah, me and mom and dad and Kevin—Mike's not here though."

"Oh." My heart rate seems to be returning to normal. As I'm turning away Andy adds, "He might be coming up later this week, though."

I'm glad my back's toward Dave so he can't see the cherry-red color I'm sure my face has just turned. I don't know what it is I'm feeling, but I'm sure I shouldn't be feeling it. Didn't I just tell myself last night that Mike McConnell means nothing to me anymore? So why am I getting all flustered over talking to his 11-year-old brother? I must be crazy.

Turning abruptly away from the craft table, I mumble something to Dave about seeing him later and head out into the gray day outside. Then I start walking—I'm not sure where, up to the area where people have their tents and trailers set up for camping. I don't even know myself what I'm searching for until I find myself staring into one campsite after another, looking at the people there, asking myself if there's anyone who could be Mike's family.

Fortunately, a glance at my watch tells me it's time to head back down to the cafeteria to start getting things ready for lunch, so I start toward the lodge. Just in time, I figure, before I find myself doing something *really* stupid, such as wandering up to total strangers and demanding "Are you Mike McConnell's dad?"

I don't see Dave anymore that afternoon, which is really good because I don't think I'd be able to fake acting normal with the way I'm feeling. Why am I so obsessed with Mike? I'd like to talk it over with one of my friends, but after the way I got burnt by Heather I'm keeping my mouth shut. Sometimes it seems like you just can't trust anyone.

I'm busy all through the afternoon, and at suppertime I join a crowded table and sit down next to Stacey. "OK, here it is," she says, beaming. "My great plan. You guys will love it, I promise."

Heather, Trevor, Bruce, Dave, and Lacey are all sitting around grinning. "Oh, no," I say. "This is the plan to set up Mr. Marsh and Mrs. Krause, right?"

"I'm sure it's gonna work," Heather declares.

"OK, tell me all about it," I say. "But I just want everyone to know this is *not* my idea!"

"Well, Thursday night, right?" Stacey begins. "Alex, you don't have to be at work till after breakfast Friday morning, and that's when everyone else's shifts start. So I figure we ask permission for all of us to canoe over to the island and camp out there overnight after campfire Thursday night. And we'll invite Mr. Marsh and Mrs. Krause to go along as chaperones. Two teachers—what could be better than that?"

"Will Pastor Howell let us go like that?" I ask.

"Oh, probably. I mean, if we're not missing any work and we're properly chaperoned," Heather says. "He was pretty cool about all that stuff last year. I mean, we do all get some time off, right?"

"First we'd better ask Mr. Marsh and Mrs. Krause if they'd be willing to come with us," Lacey says. "I mean, sure, Mr. Marsh is camp staff so that sort of makes sense, but won't Mrs. Krause get suspicious if she's invited too?"

"Not if Stacey's there," Bruce suggests. "It'll be like a chance for them to visit and catch up on all the news about music camp. I think it's a great idea, Stace. Even if it doesn't get Krause and Marsh together, it'd be fun."

The plans for the campout start falling into place that very night when Heather and Bruce, who are elected as the most responsible-seeming ones of the group, go to talk to Pastor Howell about it. Stacey tries the idea out on Mrs. Krause during campfire, and my job is to hit up Mr. Marsh, which I guess makes sense because he is like my favorite teacher. He's always making these jokes about both of us being redheads. And after the mission trip to Santa Liana, I feel pretty comfortable with him and the Edwards.

"Well, if you guys get permission from Pastor Howell and it doesn't interfere with your work, sure I'll go along," he says when I catch up to him on the way back from campfire. "Will you want Mrs. Edwards or someone to come along too? Pastor Howell might say you should have a woman along to chaperone you young girls, you know." He draws his eyebrows down low and makes his voice sound like Pastor Howell's on those last few words, which makes me laugh. But I have to kind of edge around his question.

"Um, I think Stacey's taking care of that—finding someone else to go along, I mean."

"Oh really? Who's she got in mind?"

I'd like to dodge this question altogether, but it might be even more suspicious if I don't tell him and then Mrs. Krause shows up. "Um, I think it's Mrs. Krause," I admit. "You know, I think Stacey wants to tell her all about the music camp and everything."

"Oh, right." His face brightens and I can see the idea makes him very happy. Maybe Stacey's right and there is some hope for this little teacher romance she's planning.

As for my own little romance, it looks like my mixed feelings are starting to catch up with me. I've managed to avoid being alone with Dave ever since I met Mike's brother this morning, but as I'm walking toward the washroom after talking to Mr. Marsh, I see Dave coming down the path. "Hey, Alex," he says. "Didn't see you at campfire."

41

"Oh, I was sitting with Jackie and Jared, way in the back. Must've missed you."

"Well, I missed you." He approaches close to me when he says it and gives me a big smile so there's no doubt about what he means. Dave means he missed me—really missed me, even just being apart for a few hours. I can't believe how sweet he is.

"Sorry," I say, smiling back at him in spite of myself.

"Go for a quick walk with me?" he says. "We've got a few minutes before lights-out."

"All right." I fall into step behind him as we head out the main camp road that runs toward the highway.

"You're awfully quiet," he says after a few minutes. "Penny for your thoughts."

"Believe me, they're not worth it," I say. I'm not even sure myself what I was thinking of. I don't believe it had anything to do with Mike McConnell, but I must admit I was about a million miles away. "Sounds like this campout Thursday night will be fun if we can work it out, huh?"

"Awesome," Dave agrees. "I love sleeping outdoors, don't you? Have you done a lot of camping?"

"Umm . . . not that much. My folks aren't really into taking us camping and stuff. We came up here a few times for Family Camp, but we always stayed in a cabin or a trailer," I admit.

"Oh, my family's always going camping," he says. "I just love being up in the woods."

"Yeah," I echo softly. The sky above is a velvety dark blue and the treetops are silhouetted against it in black. Stars are scattered across the blue. I'm startled when Dave asks me a question and I have to ask him to repeat it.

"Alex, are you sure there's nothing special on your mind?" he asks. "You sure have been acting weird all day."

"No—no, nothing at all!" I assure him. I think even to myself that I sound just a little too bright and cheerful.

"Because, you know, if there's something wrong, you should tell me. I mean, anything between us. Because this

42

campout—it's not going to be so great if we're not getting along, right?"

"Honestly, Dave! There's nothing wrong!" I insist.

Pausing, he glances up at the sky. "Guess we should be heading back to camp," he says. As we turn around and start back, he says, "You know what it is, Alex, I guess I'm still worried about the stuff Heather said—about you and that other guy. I'm afraid you're still thinking about him."

"No, really, I'm not, Dave. Please, please don't think about that anymore. There's nothing to it, honestly." He looks relieved, and I feel like I've got a rock planted in the middle of my stomach. I don't know how I feel about Mike, but why do I suddenly feel like I'm lying to Dave? He's being so honest, opening up and telling me what he's feeling, and here I am lying to him. Sure, right, I don't care about Mike McConnell? Then why did I spend all campfire watching little Andy McConnell and the family he was sitting with? Like I'm so obsessed with Mike I'm even obsessed with his stupid family!

Dave's got a point. Maybe this campout on Thursday night isn't going to be such a good time after all.

CHAPTER

5

We're off!" Stacey shouts, her voice rising high and excited above the lapping of waves against the shore and the roar of the speedboat's engine as it cuts in. She and Bruce, Dave and I sit behind Mr. Marsh in the boat, our camping gear piled around our feet. It's Mr. Marsh's second trip over to the island—he went over earlier with Heather, Trevor, Lacey, and Mrs. Krause. The sun is starting to slip down toward the horizon, reflected in an orange blaze on the lake. A breeze blows in off the water.

"It's so cool that Pastor Howell let us come out early, skip campfire and everything," Dave says. "And that we don't have to be back till lunchtime tomorrow."

"I know," Bruce adds. "He was pretty cool about the whole thing, I've got to admit. But after all, we do get *some* time off, and they can probably spare us better during Family Camp than any other time."

"Well, it gives us lots of time to get settled over there," Stacey says, glancing over her shoulder, across the waves to the dark silhouette of the island. "I've always wanted to spend a night out here. You OK, Alex? You're awfully quiet."

"Hmm? Oh, yeah, just excited I guess." I have really mixed feelings about this whole camping trip. For one thing, I'm still not totally comfortable with the way things are between me and Dave. And this island has a whole different set of memories for me than it does for most of my friends. Last summer, when I was working at PVA and hanging out with Tammy Doneski and all her crowd, we came up to camp for the weekend. Tammy and her friends, who were always into being tough and breaking all the rules, sneaked out to the island with all this beer and stuff, and we had a little party out there. It was the only time I ever tried drinking beer. Then I thought it was pretty cool. Now I think it's kind of stupid. But I didn't get drunk or anything. What happened was, we got caught.

I got away without too much trouble, but the school busted Tammy and some of the others. Tonight I'm a camp staffer, going over for a camping trip with all these squeaky-clean kids and two teachers as chaperones. I mean, don't get me wrong, I'm having a better time this summer than I did last summer. It's just that things have changed so much in a year, sometimes I'm not sure who I am anymore. It kind of leaves my head spinning when I think of all the stuff I've been through.

I guess Jackie was thinking of that too when I said goodbye to her in the cabin before I left. She was part of that crowd too, last summer. Since she still hangs around them, back at PVA, I think she's found this business of being camp staff and one of the "good kids" pretty hard to get used to. Jackie sort of grinned when I told her where we were going for the campout.

"The island, huh? Not like last year's party, I guess?"

"No, kinda different. Are you sure you don't—you know—don't mind not being invited?" I felt sort of awkward about that.

"Nah, I don't think Mrs. Novak could spare me off the janitorial staff tomorrow morning, with Trevor gone and all. Anyway, that's not really my crowd. Not my thing. You know."

"Yeah, I know." I looked at her once more, not sure what to say. We're friends but in a weird way. Jackie's very hard to get through to sometimes. All in all, I'm a lot more relaxed with the people on this campout than I am with any of my friends from last summer. But that doesn't explain the knotted feeling in the pit of my stomach as the speedboat cuts its engine and we pull into shore.

Dave helps me over the side of the boat and carries my knapsack—the perfect gentlemen, as always. On shore, the others already have tents set up and a fire started. "This is so *cool!*" Stacey shrieks, splashing up onto the beach.

I have to admit it is pretty cool. Tall pine trees ring the shore, pointing up against the gold and blue of the evening sky. The air is smoky from the small campfire. Heather's opening a bag of marshmallows, and Lacey and Trevor return from the woods with sticks for marshmallow roasting. "This is going to be the girls' tent over here," says Mrs. Krause, sticking her head out of a tent flap. "You can put your things in here, Alex." Wearing cutoff shorts and a T-shirt and her hair up in a ponytail, she looks really young and pretty. After this whole summer at camp I've gotten pretty used to seeing Mr. and Mrs. Edwards and Mr. Marsh dressed casually—I was used to that, anyway, after the Santa Liana mission trip— but seeing any other teacher in jeans or shorts still gives me a shock. I keep forgetting they're like human beings on their time off.

Mr. Marsh is alone in the speedboat now, revving it up again to return to camp alone. We can't keep the speedboat out overnight because camp will need it in the morning, and we can't take too many canoes for the same reason. So Mr. Marsh is going back to drop off the speedboat and pick up a canoe.

"You sure you can manage bringing the canoe back alone, Mr. Marsh?" Stacey says. "Someone could go with you."

"Yeah, I could go," Bruce adds, but Stacey gives him a sharp dig in the ribs.

"Maybe you could go, Mrs. Krause," Stacey says sweetly.

I roll my eyes. How obvious can she get? But Mr. Marsh and Mrs. Krause look at each other with this private teachery sort of smile and Mr. Marsh says, "No, I think I'll be OK."

When he's pulled away from the beach, Mrs. Krause says

with a grin, "What were you trying to do, Stacey, get rid of both your chaperones before the campout's even started?" You can tell she's joking, but Stacey blushes really pink.

"Oh, no, Mrs. Krause, I wasn't thinking that at all!" she mumbles. Fortunately she doesn't say anymore than that. I hope Mrs. Krause thinks that's *all* Stacey's up to.

With my stuff safely stowed in the girls' tent, I sit down on the sand near the fire. It's almost sunset now. I take a marshmallow from the bag Heather offers me and skewer it on a stick. This is the first evening in weeks I haven't been in the middle of a big crowd, usually involving lots of screaming kids. It's so peaceful out here. The water spashes against the shore, the fire crackles, birds call. Everything seems all right.

Dave sits down beside me as I'm trying to get my marshmallow to turn a nice brown. "I always burn one side of it," I complain.

"Here, want me to do one for you?" he asks.

"Sure, OK." I'm not really into this big-he-man-does-everything-better act, but Dave's not like that. If he thinks he can toast my marshmallow better than I can, that's OK. I hand him the stick and lean back on the ground, staring up at the sky. It's so hard not to compare tonight with that other night last summer—another warm, beautiful evening. We had a fire then, but it wasn't so peaceful because some of the guys had a stereo cranked up with all this heavy-metal music. I had a guy beside me, too, but not one as nice as Dave—it was Walt, my dumb geeky friend Walt. Guess I shouldn't think of him that way. He's been a pretty good friend to me during this past year. I didn't know it back then, but he had a crush on me— did for a long time. I think he's gotten over it by now. I hope. I could never think of Walt that way!

But that night last summer, I was so lonely and so desperate to be "wild," I almost ended up kissing him. I don't know if I really would have done it—we got busted before I had a chance to find out. But I was definitely flirting with him. Don't ask me what made me that crazy.

Dave hands me the stick with my marshmallow on it, the

marshmallow toward me so I can pop it in my mouth. "Careful," he says, "it's hot."

It is, too, and it's a perfect golden-brown all over. "You are good at this," I tell him.

"Anything for you, my lady," he says, joking but also serious, I can tell. Then he kisses me quickly, marshmallow and all. It's just a quick peck, but I'm startled because, you know, Mrs. Krause being here and everything. I mean, this is one party I *wasn't* expecting to turn into a make-out session, with teachers along for chaperones. But a quick glance assures me that Mrs. Krause is deep in conversation with Stacey. I look back at Dave and in the flickering glow of the firelight his face is so good-looking I almost wish this *was* going to be a make-out kind of party.

As I chew my marshmallow and settle into the warmth of Dave's company, I have to remember—I can't help remembering—the other thing about last summer. Which was, of course, Mike McConnell. *He* was the reason I was desparate enough to flirt with Walt Rubenik. Mike and I had been dating, then he dumped me and came up here to camp to get back together with Sheena Alvarez. They've been on-again-off-again for a long time—for all I know they might be together again now. But last summer, when Mike dumped me, I thought the world was coming to an end. And that's really why I feel so weird about being out on this island with all my new friends—with Dave especially. Because just being in this place brings back that feeling so strong and clear I could almost cry all over again. Especially knowing that Mike's still, somehow, thinking of me. And I'm still thinking of him.

"You're deep in thought," Dave says, dragging my attention back to him and the present.

"Oh—sorry. Just—you know, daydreaming."

"You're doing a lot of that lately." His voice is steady, but I know he's ticked off because I'm not giving him my full attention. I bet he still thinks it has something to do with Mike. I hope he never finds out how right he is.

But the splash of paddles offshore breaks the tension, and

48

we all look out to see the canoe gliding toward us across the water. Even in the twilight semi-darkness, it's easy to see that there's two people in it, not one. Mr. Marsh in the back, and someone else in the front.

"Who else is coming over?" Stacey asks, a frown on her forehead. The whole campout is her big plan, and I guess she can't stand the thought of anyone ruining it. Myself, I don't think she should be so snobbish. If Mr. Marsh picked up some other kid who wanted to come along, why not bring him or her?

"Oh, that's my friend Kate," Mrs. Krause says. "You remember—Miss Nichol? She's staying up here with my parents and me."

"Oh," Stacey replies, and flashes me a look that says *Oh NO!* Another adult female—that totally throws off everything. It's not like there's anything wrong with Mrs. Krause's friend or anything. She's an English teacher at some other academy—not PVA—and I met her once before when she visited Mrs. Krause. She's about the same age as Mrs. Krause and Mr. Marsh and, for a teacher, she seems pretty nice. But she's definitely not going to help with Stacey's plan for getting Mr. Marsh and Mrs. Krause alone together.

They're almost onto the beach now. Mr. Marsh and Kate get out and pull the canoe up onshore together, then join us around the campfire. He introduces Kate Nichol to the kids who don't know her, and she sits down between him and Mrs. Krause. She whispers something to Mrs. Krause, and they start giggling together—just like I would with Stacey or Heather or any of my friends. It's always weird when teachers act like teenagers, when you see them with their own friends and stuff. Suddenly I'm struck by this thought— could it be that Mrs. Krause *knows* what we're up to? That she doesn't like Mr. Marsh—not in a romantic way, anyway—and she doesn't want to get set up with him? In that case, it would make a lot of sense for her to bring her friend along—kind of as protection. I know there are lots of times I've dragged one of my girlfriends along when Walt wanted to go somewhere with me,

49

just to make it a threesome so he wouldn't get any ideas. Maybe that's what Mrs. Krause is up to.

But I don't have a lot of time to stew over the romantic lives of old people, because Stacey's trying to teach everyone a game she learned at music camp—one that reminds me of charades only more embarrassing, if that's possible. To my surprise, when I finally get dragged in, it is kind of fun. Soon we're all laughing like idiots. In the middle of all this, Lacey runs down to the beach to get away from Trevor and Heather who are chasing her for some reason. She grabs up a paper cup and flicks water in Trevor's face, and suddenly it's this big free-for-all water fight. I half expect the teachers to try to stop it, but they just sit there laughing while we get each other drenched. When Dave lets fly with a washpan full of water right in Mr. Marsh's face, Mr. Marsh jumps up and joins right in.

Soon I'm soaked to the skin and shivering, but laughing too, as Dave chases me down the beach with his washpan once again full. It's a good thing we all brought extra clothes or we'd all get pneumonia tonight, sleeping out after this. After running a little ways I let Dave catch me and soak me, because water fights can be fun with a guy you like. I wonder if Stacey's thought of that possibility for dragging Mr. Marsh and Mrs. Krause together, but a glance up the beach shows me Mrs. Krause and Kate both pouring water over Mr. Marsh. Since the teachers are so well occupied, and we're down at the far end of the island beach, Dave takes the opportunity to kiss me again. This time it's a little longer and little more romantic—no marshmallow, more privacy and everything.

"I wish we were out here all by ourselves," he says suddenly.

I'm totally taken by surprise. "Well, that's not very likely to happen, is it?" I say, then wish I'd said something just a little more romantic.

"I know, I know. It's just—we hardly ever have any time alone together." He steps back a little, looking at me seriously. "I mean, I know that's good in a way, because we've really gotten to know each other without just making out and stuff. But sometimes I'd like there to be more 'and stuff.' Now that we do know each other."

For the moment I'm speechless, which anyone can tell you doesn't happen very often. I must look great, just standing there with my mouth hanging open. Dave gets the wrong idea about why I'm so dumbstruck and rushes in to explain, stumbling over his words like big clumsy feet.

"Oh, I mean I . . . I don't mean . . . you know. I mean I don't want to go too far or get in trouble or anything," he says, blushing just at the thought. "I mean . . . I really care about you, Alex. I'd like to get more serious."

Finally I've got to say something. "Well, Dave . . . I . . . I feel the same way. I do. But . . . but like we said before, what's the point of getting serious? It's just this summer and then we'll be miles apart all school year." Even while I'm saying it my heart is pounding and my feelings are telling me, *Go for it! Who cares about next year?*

"I'm not so sure about that," Dave says. "I've been talking to my folks. There's some chance they might send me to PVA this coming year, if I really want it."

"Really?" This changes everything. I've got to think, but there's no time. Already I can hear Mrs. Krause's voice up the beach, calling everyone back. Maybe the other couples have wandered away too. "Dave . . . that'd be great. But . . . I don't know . . ."

"Well, nothing's settled yet." He glances behind him up the beach. "We should head back," he says, then turns back to me and gives me a very definite kiss, as if to seal what he's said. I feel like my cheeks are still glowing bright red when we walk back to the campsite.

Naturally, it's the teachers who are acting sensible now, getting everyone together, herding us into the tents to change into dry clothes and building up the fire so we can get warm again. When we're all back around the fire, Stacey and Mrs. Krause start singing. Mr. Marsh breaks out his guitar, and we all join in. It's the same songs we sing at campfire every night, but they feel different somehow, here with just a small

51

group of close friends. I relax into drowsiness and let my head droop against Dave's shoulder. All the things he said are whirling around my head. Wanting to get more serious—coming to PVA next year—wishing we had more time together—it all makes me feel so good inside that the memory of last summer, and of Mike McConnell, seems as faraway as a dream.

Soon after that we crawl into our sleeping bags and drift off to sleep. The next thing I know it's morning, with the first light of dawn and the first songs of the birds, and we're all up and into our swimsuits in time for an early swim. Afterward we cook breakfast, which seems to take forever over the open fire, but it is really a lot of fun. Finally, reluctantly, we start packing up. Like all fun trips, our campout seems to have lasted much longer than the few hours it really did, and it's hard to believe the camp is just a short boatride away. For one night, we've been in our own private world.

Mr. Marsh leaves with the canoe—this time he takes Bruce with him—and they return a little later in the speedboat, ready to ferry us to camp. "Everything was perfect," Stacey sighs on the way back. Then she cuts her voice so it's lower than the roar of the engine. "Except our little plan. I hardly saw Marsh and Krause talking to each other the whole evening, did you?"

"Not really. Maybe a little. They were fooling around and stuff in the water fight last night."

"Yeah, but that was all three of them—Mrs. Krause's friend was with them the whole time. Why'd they have to bring *her* along?"

I sigh. "You know, Stacey, sometimes you just have to let people run their *own* lives. After all, they are adults. Maybe they're just not interested in each other!"

Stacey shakes her head. "They're *perfect* for each other," she insists, frowning, and I can see she's cooking up yet another scheme.

Almost as soon as we're on the campgrounds it's back to work, which for me means the kitchen to start getting supper ready. "So, was it a good campout?" my coworker Doretha asks as we peel vegetables together.

"Oh, it was great," I tell her.

Lacey, on my other side, says, "*Really* great for Alex!"

"What's that supposed to mean?" I ask. "You had a good time too, didn't you?"

"Oh, sure, but I wasn't doing the Romeo and Juliet thing, if you know what I mean." She grins. "Come on, I was watching you and Dave. That was one romantic evening!"

I smile in spite of myself. "Well, no need to be jealous. We *could* have asked Jared along, you know!"

"Oh, give me a break! Come on now, am I right? Was it all romantic and lovey-dovey?"

"We didn't get that much chance to be alone—but yeah. Yeah, it was." I smile again, and Lacey gives me a big thumbs-up sign. I think it's safe now for me to start telling my friends that Dave and I are officially going out. Especially if he might be at PVA this fall. After the things he said last night, there can't be much doubt anymore.

It's only an hour or two later that I'm standing behind the counter, serving in the supper line, and my world turns upside down again. I'm ladling hash browns onto people's plates when a familiar voice—too familiar—catches my ear. I glance up and there, at the back of the line, is a tall, broad-shouldered figure I can't possibly miss. It's been a while since I've seen him, but for me, Mike McConnell will always stand out in any crowd.

In the second between seeing him and him noticing me, my stomach does a flip-flop, and I realize I've missed the plate I'm supposed to be filling and dumped hash browns on the counter. "Sorry," I say, scrambling to scoop up more, and by the time I glance up again, Mike's looking away. Now I'm not even sure he's actually seen me.

But he's coming through line, and everything I suddenly thought was so secure and so settled in my mind—stuff about me and Dave—is swept away with one glance from his brown eyes. Only he doesn't look at me any more—not till the very last minute, when he's standing with his plate in front of me. It's been only two weeks since I received that letter saying he was still thinking of me, but all he does now is nod. He doesn't say hi or anything, not even when I manage to squeak out, "Hi, Mike." Not a smile, not a word, nothing. Before I've fully registered that he's there, he's gone, moving down the line, heading out into the dining hall without so much as a backward glance.

Mechanically I go through the motions of filling plates and smiling and stuff, but it's like my brain has melted. *I can't stand this. How can he come through here and not even say hi to me? How long is he up here for? Is he mad that I didn't answer his letter?* A million questions swirl through my mind, and one of the most important ones is, *What on earth is going to happen to me and Dave* now?

CHAPTER

6

Mike McConnell is a jerk.

I don't know why I'm lying awake in my bunk here, trying to think up complicated explanations for why he's showed up here at camp only to ignore me. The explanation is actually quite simple. It's been staring me in the face for a year. He's a jerk, and he likes to mess with people's heads. That's all there is to it.

So if he's a jerk, why can't I get over him?

All around me I hear the sounds of the other girls breathing softly in their sleep—well, not all that softly. Vanessa snores a little, although of course she swears she doesn't. We should tape her sometime. Everyone's peacefully sleeping, except for me, lying awake worrying about why Mike McConnell's suddenly not speaking to me.

It's not as if I'm not used to getting the silent treatment from him. After we kind of broke up last summer, he hardly talked to me for most of the fall and winter. It was as if I just didn't exist, even though I was still crazy about him. I spent almost all of last summer staring at Mike McConnell's back while he walked across campus with one girl or another. Then, when the ice started to thaw down in Santa Liana, it was as if he knew who I was again. Even though he was back with Sheena at the time, he began talking to me, and for the rest of the year it was as if we were actually friends again. He and Sheena broke up right before school let out, and he was even friendlier then. Only I was finally starting to get over him—especially once I came up here and met Dave. Until I got that stupid, stupid note.

Why would a guy send me a note like that and then totally ignore me? Is he that much of a jerk? The question pounds over and over in my head until I think I'll go crazy if I can't ask it out loud to someone, even though I know no one has the answer.

Rolling out of my sleeping bag, I shove my feet into my sneakers, pull a sweatshirt over my head, and go silently—I hope—out the cabin door and onto the front step. It's after midnight and the whole campground is quiet—more quiet even than usual, since it's Friday night and that Sabbath-y feeling has spread over the place. Maybe because it's Sabbath, my question turns into kind of a prayer. I never used to pray much—in fact I didn't think much about God at all since I felt He'd given me a lousy deal with the family I got stuck in and everything. But this year things have changed. I wouldn't say I'm a super-holy person, like maybe my friend Dana is, but I have started to think about God. I've gotten used to talking to Him about things. But I'm not sure if you're supposed to bother Him with stuff like this. I mean, guy stuff—that's not really covered a whole lot in the Bible. It's kind of embarassing—and also, I couldn't really be sure God would approve of me and Mike. Mike's pretty wild. I could see God wanting to get me together with a nice Christian guy like Dave, but Mike's a whole different story.

All the same, the words are whirling around in my brain and no one's there but God to listen to them. "What's the problem with Mike?" I whisper. "Or what's the problem with *me?* Why does he keep rejecting me and treating me like dirt?

I really do care about him . . . I think." Perhaps it's not so much that I care about him—maybe I just want the chance to find out. Maybe I want the chance to get to know him without getting dumped right away for the next pretty girl that comes along. I think—I've always thought—that there's a sweet, sensitive guy inside Mike's tough-guy shell. He's so hung up on being cool and popular, but I know there are things that really hurt him, and I wish he'd talk to me about them. I believe I could help him.

I don't say any of this out loud, but I guess God knows it's going through my mind. I just keep coming back to the way Mike looked walking away from me in the cafeteria tonight, hardly even glancing my way. And all evening—it seemed as if I kept seeing him over and over, at campfire and afterward, and he never once said hi. I saw him talking to other PVA people, but he didn't have a word for me. He was even speaking to Jackie. Maybe he asked her about me, but why didn't he talk to me? Again I clench my fists and whisper, "How big a jerk can he be?"

I don't know if it's because I've been talking to God or what, but the next thought that pops into my head isn't a very comfortable one. It's the thought of Dave on the beach last night—was it only last night?—saying he might be coming to PVA and maybe we should get a little more serious. Oh wow. And all evening tonight I sat next to Dave at campfire, not even seeing or hearing him, obsessed with Mike. And the question I can't get out of my head is: *How big of a jerk can I be?*

Apparently the answer to that is, "A really major jerk," because although I feel guilty as anything about it, nothing's changed the next morning. I'm crabby from my nearly sleepness night, Dave is still being sweet although I'm practically ignoring him, and as far as Mike's concerned I don't exist. I spot him again in youth Sabbath school—not inside the lodge, where the program's being held, but hanging out on the steps, as you might expect cool Mike McConnell to be doing—and he doesn't even notice me.

I've borrowed this really nice white skirt—a full pleated

skirt that comes just above the knee, with a gold belt buckle—from Heather, and a blue blouse from Vanessa, and I got up early to wash my hair while the shower was still hot so I could make sure it looked really nice. From what I saw in the bathroom mirror, I have to admit I don't think I look half bad, and I usually think I look about three-quarters bad, with the frizzy red hair and everything. Today it looks smooth and coppery-shiny, the way I want it to, and the blue-green of the shirt highlights my eyes, while the white skirt shows that I actually do have a nice tan on my legs. All in all, I'm pleased with the results.

Dave is too. He says, "Hey, you look great this morning," when I enter the lodge for Sabbath school. But Mike? I walked right under his nose and he didn't even give me a second glance. I don't want it to matter, but there's a burning knot right in the pit of my stomach that I know will be there until he talks to me.

We have a trip to a wildlife park in the afternoon, but I'm working in the cafe, and to tell you the truth, I'm not a bit sorry. Dave is free and going on the trip—so are a lot of my friends—but I don't think I could handle it. I don't want to spend anymore time with Dave than I have to, feeling like the traitor I am. And if Mike went along, and was still ignoring me, it'd just about drive me crazy.

When my shift ends just after supper, I head back to the cabin to change. Jackie's there, sprawled on the bunk like she's just coming out of a long nap.

"How was the trip to the nature park?" I ask. "Did you go?"

Jackie nods and says around a yawn, "Wasn't going to, but Jared and Nancy dragged me along. It was OK. Mike McConnell was there—had a talk with him."

"Yeah?" I try to make my voice as casual as it can possibly be given that my heart is racing like a runaway train.

"Yeah. You been talking to him yet?"

"No, not really. Just to say hi. Why, what's he up to?"

I don't know if I'm fooling Jackie or not. She knows I liked Mike last year, about the letter, and everything. I guess I'm not fooling her.

But she just gives this kind of a snorty laugh. "Mike. Honestly, you know who should be together? Mike and Tammy. They're two of a kind."

"Mike McConnell and Tammy Doneski?" It is not exactly what I want to hear right now. "They'd scratch each other's eyes out in 10 minutes."

"Yeah, maybe—but would that be so bad? No, I mean, it's just the same old story from both of them. What a big party it is being down in Lemoine over the summer and living off campus. I heard it all last summer from Evan and Gary—they were off campus then—but it's even worse with Mike because he has to be such a big shot and show off so much, bragging about getting drunk and everything. It's so childish."

The weird thing with Jackie is that you can never tell whether she really thinks something is wrong or right. I don't even know if she drinks much herself or anything—I know she tried it last summer, just like I did, but I never saw her drunk. But she's definitely not into playing the good Christian role either. She just seems to think the whole Lemoine party scene is kind of boring now.

But this isn't what I want to hear about Mike either. It disappoints me to hear he's still into partying, but, let's be honest, that's part of what makes him so exciting. I know he only does it because he's really unhappy, and if things would just work out for him, he'd settle down. I'd just like to be the one who makes things work out. "So, is that all he was saying? About partying and stuff?"

"Oh, he had all kinds of gossip about everyone—it's kind of strange he hasn't been talking to you, isn't it?"

With my back to her as I stare out the doorway, I shrug. "Don't ask me. I'm not the one with my nose in the air."

"Oh, is that it? He's ignoring you?"

"Sort of, I guess."

Jackie laughs again. "Come on, Alex, you're not dumb enough to fall for that act, are you? He's just trying to appear like a big shot so you'll fall all over yourself getting him to notice you. Tell him to go jump in the lake—there's a nice big one right over there."

"Very funny. So he didn't—say anything about me, did he?" I'm dying with shame just asking it, but I've got to know. Life can't go on otherwise.

"Sure he did. Wanted to know if you were going out with that nerdy looking blond wimp. His words, not mine."

I *hate* the way that makes me feel! I'm actually happy he insulted Dave, even though it's a terrible thing to say. Mike must still like me, if he's going around making rude remarks about the guy I'm dating. How totally, totally shallow of me.

"Well, he's still pretty full of himself, isn't he? I don't know where he gets off talking about Dave like that—what did you tell him?"

"Told him I didn't know. You know my motto—keep your nose out of other people's business."

Unlike most people I know at PVA—and at camp— Jackie is actually pretty good at living up to her motto. She's not a person you'd go to for advice or to get her to give some guy a message for you. Instead she's always saying, "You're a big girl, handle it yourself." It can seem kind of cold sometimes, but when I think of the way my friends at academy are always getting involved in people's lives and making things worse—like Heather when she told Dave I was still interested in Mike—I have to admire Jackie's hands-off policy.

But the Saturday night activities—which include a hayride, a scavenger hunt, and a big talent show, all of which would be loads of fun if I were in a good mood—slip by, and although I keep running into Mike, it's obvious that I've turned into The Invisible Woman. There's no way this is just some accident—he is really, truly ignoring me. I try to spend the whole evening surrounded by a crowd and not get alone with Dave, because I know he recognizes by now that something's up. Someone must have tipped him off that Mike is the guy I liked at PVA—or else he's just figured it out for himself, which wouldn't be hard, given the weird way I've been acting.

Falling into bed exhausted, I wish the whole day hadn't

happened. But what occurs on Sunday morning is even weirder. Everyone's piling into vans, cars, and campers, getting ready to leave. A bunch of us—Heather, Bruce, Trevor, Lacey, me—are up in the parking lot saying goodbye to Stacey, who's driving off with her family. As we turn to go back to camp, I see Mike leaning on the hood of his dad's truck, staring straight at me.

Although I try to look past him, as he's been doing to me all weekend, he catches my eye, definitely staring at me. "So, Alex," he says. "How's it been going?"

I can hardly find my voice. Some part of me wants to ignore him, to keep on walking, but my feet slow down all on their own, and I find myself standing across from him, saying, "Not bad, I guess."

"Enjoy working up here?"

"It's OK. Yeah, I like it."

"It's boring back in Lemoine. Slaving away at the woodwork."

"I know. You wrote me a letter."

"I did? Oh yeah—so I did. A couple of weeks ago, right?"

"That's right." He *forgot* about the letter? Yeah *right!*

"I'm not usually much of a letter writer," he says.

"Yeah, I know. I was so flattered to get one from you." I hope my voice sounds sarcastic. It's supposed to.

"Coming back to PVA next year?"

"Sure—I guess so. That's what I'm earning all this money for." I can't believe how smooth and level my voice sounds. "Why, aren't you?"

"Dunno. I don't want to go back home to Wilcox, that's for sure. Just the weekend with the old man nearly drove me nuts. I might stay in Lemoine and attend Regional."

"Yeah, that's what Tammy's doing, isn't it?" I think about what Jackie said about Tammy and Mike being perfect for each other. Maybe there's something going on there.

But Mike says, "Is it? I don't know, I don't see that much of her. She's so psycho, she doesn't know what she's doing from one minute to the next. I don't know about going back

61

to academy. It's better than nothing."

He's so positive. Honestly, why do I like this guy? I'm certainly *not* going to stand here and talk him into returning to PVA, if that's what he wants. Let him live his own life. "Well, I'm going back. I had a good year last year." *In spite of you,* I feel like adding.

"Well, if you're going back, that makes it look a little better," he says with a crooked grin that totally reminds me exactly why I like him. "Anyway, gotta go. See you back at the Peeve." That's the nickname we have for PVA. Without even saying goodbye, he walks away, his steady, long-legged strides covering the ground quickly.

I'm left there with my heart pounding and my stomach doing flip-flops. He strung me out the whole weekend just to give me this one little thrill at the end, and I can't even feel angry at him for it. I'm just so happy—so happy—we finally talked and he wants to see me back at PVA next year. For just a minute, as I race toward the cafeteria where work is calling me, I feel like everything in the world is perfect again.

It's about two minutes before I remember Dave; before I remember that everything is not perfect. What should I do— break up with Dave? Tell him I don't want to see him anymore? That would be pretty stupid, based on one conversation with a guy who's been a total jerk for so long. But unless I want to be a jerk too, it's what I might have to do.

I still feel like I need someone to talk to, but I'm not about to trust Heather again, and Jackie's made it totally clear she doesn't want to get involved. For a wild minute I even think about Mrs. Edwards. But I'm not one of those people to go spilling my guts to a teacher, even though I get along pretty well with the teachers who are up here this summer. Lots of girls see Mrs. Edwards for advice on all sorts of stuff, but that's not me.

But, to my surprise, when I do get some advice, it actually does come from a teacher, though I don't ask for it. And it's not Mrs. Edwards. It's Mr. Marsh, who I probably get along with best of all my teachers, though I wouldn't exactly think of going to him for advice on my love life. I mean, him being a man and all, it would be even worse than talking to Mrs. Edwards. But the conversation just comes up so naturally, I don't even have to ask.

It's late Sunday afternoon and I'm down at the waterfront, just off work and back from a quick trip around the lake on waterskis. A few more people line up to go, just staffers because the next batch of campers haven't arrived yet. The camp that starts tonight is horsemanship camp, so we don't expect the waterfront to be too busy over the next week. Right now some of the staff are just relaxing, but it's pretty quiet down here. Mr. Edwards and Josh are in the boat, and Mr. Marsh is sitting on the dock, lifeguarding I guess.

"How's it going, Alex?" he says as I sit down near him.

"Oh, pretty good," I say in a voice that doesn't let on any hint of the churning swirl of emotions going around in my head.

"That was a lot of fun, that campout Thursday night," he says. "Nice of you guys to pick me as one of your chaperones."

"Oh, no problem. I mean, we knew you wouldn't give us any hassle as long as we didn't give you any." I'm not about to let on about the other reason for choosing him, which seems to have been a total failure. Mrs. Krause is gone now, along with everyone else from Family Camp, and I can't remember seeing him alone with her anytime over the weekend. Although I'll have to admit my thoughts were somewhere else most of the time.

"I'm glad you asked Angie too," he says, a comment that makes no sense until I clue in that he's talking about Mrs. Krause, whose first name is Angela. "The teachers who don't spend their summers up here at camp sometimes envy those of us who do, because we have a chance to get closer to you kids. I think she enjoyed that."

"Good," I say. "Anyway, Stacey planned it all, and of course she would ask Mrs. Krause—she's her favorite teacher."

"And don't worry, no one's going to go asking you who *your* favorite teacher is," he grins.

"Oh, Mr. Stevens, of course, because I love math so much!" I shoot back.

He leans back and stares at the sky, his voice faraway as if he's not really paying attention to me at all, just talking out loud. "It was fun, though, to get away from here and spend a little while with some of you kids, and with my own friends too. Angie and Kate and I are really close friends; we go back a long ways."

"Really? Even before you taught at PVA?"

"Even before then, back in prehistory," he says. "In ancient times, when we all wrote in hieroglyphics and stuff."

"Yeah, right! You know how it is; we just can't imagine any of you teachers having actual lives of your own."

"Believe it or not, we do. And there's a lot to be said for getting together with old friends."

I nod. "There sure is. Although some of my old friends I don't fit in with so well anymore."

He looks back at me. "That's the problem, isn't it? You change, people change, you're not sure if you really belong together anymore. Although sometimes—sometimes you can change and grow closer to an old friend, instead of farther away from them."

"I guess that's true." I stare at my knee, picking a scab that's miraculously appeared there.

"The thing is," Mr. Marsh adds, "sometimes you think you might have had a chance to be *more* than friends with someone, and then you go in different directions and you never find out."

Instantly I look up from my knee to him. He must be a *lot* more observant than I'd thought, if he knows about my whole thing with Mike. But he couldn't make it much more obvious without embarassing me. "That's true," I say. "What are you supposed to do when that happens?"

"I don't know," he says. That's a cool thing about Mr. Marsh—he says "I don't know" when he doesn't know the answer, which a lot of teachers will never do; not in class or even just in a conversation like this. Is it such a crime to admit you don't have all the answers, just because you're an adult? "Most people would say forget it and get on with your life. I'm not sure that's always the best advice."

"No?"

"Who knows? But sometimes I think— I've just got a feeling sometimes you've got to go for it; to take a chance on something even if you don't know it'll work out. Otherwise, you could spend your whole life wondering and probably kicking yourself!"

"Yeah, well, I do plenty of that!" I tell him.

"Is that where you got all those bruises—or is that from waterskiing?" he says, and just like that the conversation returns to our ordinary teasing thing, talking about waterskiing and other sports, and what horsemanship camp is going to be like. After a few minutes he wanders off and speaks to someone else. But he's left me with a lot to think about. Mr. Marsh is always fooling around and not acting serious, except in class. But in spite of his joking I have a lot of respect for him because he's the one adult who made me think seriously about God, down in Santa Liana this spring, because he was honest with me about what God can do in a person's life. And before that all I'd seen from adults—even my own parents— seemed to just be hypocrisy. Now I know there are other adults who are real Christians and can be honest about it—the Edwards, Pastor Howell, even my mom now that we've finally started speaking to each other. But since Mr. Marsh was the first one, I tend to listen to him.

And what's he been telling me? Without even seeming like he's giving advice, he told me the one thing I most needed to hear—go for it. Give it a shot, or I'll never know what would have happened between me and Mike. And I don't want to spend the rest of my life wishing I'd found out.

CHAPTER

7

Horsemanship camp. Well, it's certainly different from the other camps we've had up here. All the action is up at the stables, there's a smaller group of kids, and they're all these really keeners—little kids anxious to win blue ribbons and stuff. But for me, it's much the same as any other camp. No matter what people are doing up here, they still have to be fed, don't they? So I'm stuck cooking in the kitchen just like always.

If I sound a little depressed—OK, a *lot* depressed—it's because this is the worst week of the whole summer. There's nothing wrong with horses and horsey kids, don't get me wrong. And the weather's a little rainier than it's been most of the summer, but that's not really the problem either. The problem is with me. I'm messing things up between Dave and me, and I can't stand it.

After Family Camp, I'm totally convinced Mike's still interested in me. Otherwise, why would he be playing stupid mind games with me? A year ago I would have thought having two guys on the string was the most exciting thing that could happen to me. I used to daydream about it when I first went to PVA. But the reality's not fun at all. The reality is seeing the look in Dave's eyes as day after day I push him farther away, make excuses not to go for a walk or a canoe ride with him, talk to him less and less. By the middle of the week I can tell he's starting to get mad at me.

"I need to get away from here!" I tell Jackie in the cabin on Tuesday night. "This place is just driving me crazy!"

"So go home for a weekend," she says. "You haven't had a weekend off yet, have you?"

"No." I could do that. But as soon as I think about Fairview and my parents' house, I know that's not where I want to go. "That'd be boring. My folks would drive me crazy. I don't know, maybe I could call Dana, see if I could visit her for the weekend. Or—or I could go back to the academy. You know, a lot of people are staying there for the summer. Perhaps I could go back and visit in the dorm for a weekend."

"Oh-ho!" says Jackie. "So *that's* what this is all about. You don't want to get away from camp; you just want to get back to Lemoine and see if Mike McConnell is going to pay any attention to you, don't you?"

"Jackie! No way! I just want—I just—I don't know!" In frustration I slap my pillow down on the bunk. The door opens and Liesl and Vanessa spill into the room, talking and giggling, which cuts off my conversation with Jackie. Liesl, who sees herself in a big sister role of looking out for me, thinks Dave and I are perfect together. She doesn't mind Mike—she gets along with him, like most people do—but I know she considers him a big flirt. Sheena, his ex-girlfriend, is one of Liesl's good friends, and for a lot of reasons I know she wouldn't approve of me getting mixed up with Mike again. And I'm definitely not going to talk about it in front of her.

The next morning I find myself asking Pastor Howell if I can have the weekend off. "To go home?" he asks.

For a minute I think of just saying yes, but I know the camp is pretty careful about checking up on staff when they leave for overnight, making sure they're not just taking off to somewhere they're not supposed to. "No, Pastor Howell, I want to go back to the academy for the weekend. I have—um, some of my friends are working there for the summer, and I thought I'd just like to visit them."

"Well, as long as it's OK with your parents," he says. "You'll have to call and check. Or get Mrs. Edwards to call. She's the girls' director and will have to know what your plans are."

"Sure thing, Pastor." I don't know what my folks will say about me going to Lemoine for the weekend. Maybe if I'm lucky I'll get my mom at home instead of my dad. Since he's gone back to work at the hardware store after his heart attack, and she's off school for the summer, I figure telephoning during the day is a pretty good bet, even though it's more expensive.

In fact, that's the first thing Mom points out when I call from the camp office. "Julie!" she says—my whole family calls me Julie—Alex is my school nickname. "What are you doing phoning in the middle of the day? Is something wrong?"

"No, Mom, I just want to take a weekend off next weekend, and I need your permission to go down to PVA and stay in the dorm, OK?" Sure. Like it's going to be that simple.

"My goodness, Julie, you could have waited till this evening to save us some money . . . oh well, never mind. How are you? Is everything going all right?"

"Yes, yes, everything's great. Mom, what about the weekend? Can I go down to PVA?"

"Well, dear, if you've got the weekend off, why don't you come home here? We'd love to have you; we haven't seen you since school ended."

Guilt, guilt, guilt. I really ought to go home. "No, Mom, I mean, camp will be over in another couple weeks and then I'll be home for a week before school starts. I'd just like to go down to PVA and stay in the dorm this weekend, OK?"

"Well . . . I suppose so. I don't know if your dad will think . . . "

"Mom, it's the *dorm*. It's *supervised*. I just want to see some of my friends."

"Well, all right then . . . "

"Good, can you tell Mrs. Edwards I've got permission? She's right here."

So it's all settled. I can catch a ride with some other staff members—some of the college kids—who are driving down to Lemoine for the weekend, and I can stay in the dorm. My friend Shantelle, Jackie's roommate, is still in the dorm over the summer, and I guess she'll let me crash on her floor.

The decision to go to Lemoine makes me feel a little better. At least I'll get my head straightened out about this Mike thing once and for all. Once I'm down there, it shouldn't be hard to look him up and have a talk with him. Just to find out what he's thinking. If there's really a chance for us . . . well, I don't know what I'll do. I might have to break up with Dave. I just don't know. But after this weekend, I should know, one way or another.

"You're looking a little more cheerful." Dave says when he sees me at supper. It's the very end of suppertime, when I've finished serving in line and almost everyone's gone. I carry my tray out to a table, thinking I'll sit alone, but Dave's been waiting for me.

"Oh, yeah. Well, I'm getting this weekend off."

Right away I know it was a mistake to say this. His face lights right up. "Hey, really? Are you going home?" I barely have time to shake my head before he says, "I wonder if it's too late for me to get the weekend off too? We could go down to my place, like we talked about. My folks would love to meet you. Would you like to come down?"

Oh no. I feel like somebody who drowns kittens for a living. This is terrible. "Uh—yeah, Dave, I'd like to—I mean, I know I said I'd like to, but could it be some other time? Because, well, I've got plans already for this weekend."

His face falls. "Oh. Well, OK. Who are you going to visit?"

"I'm going back to PVA, to stay in the dorm for the weekend," I say miserably. I can tell by the way his forehead wrinkles into a frown that he knows right away that it involves Mike. But he doesn't say anything. Literally, not anything. Instead he just gets up, takes his tray, and says, "Well,

I hope you have a good weekend." Which is a weird thing to say when you realize it's only Wednesday.

But maybe it's not so weird, because for the rest of the week I hardly see Dave. First it was me avoiding him, but now it's definitely him avoiding me. I feel lost and empty, like a part of me's been cut off. I didn't realize how used I was getting to Dave and his company. He's not rude or anything, he just doesn't have a whole lot to say whenever I'm around him, and he doesn't ask me to go out in the canoe anymore, or make any special effort to sit next to me at campfire.

If I've thrown away Dave Vickers for Mike McConnell, Mike had better be worth it.

On Friday afternoon I'm still hoping Dave will show up to say goodbye before I leave the campgrounds, but I'm not really expecting him to. I don't really deserve it, I guess. But just as I'm throwing my knapsack in the back of Josh's car, I see Dave heading down the trail to the parking lot. Maybe it's just coincidence that he came by here right now, but I'm still glad when he wanders over and nods, hands in his pockets. "See ya, Alex. Have a nice weekend."

"You too, Dave." He's told me he's going home anyway. Going home without me. For one second I want to grab my knapsack back and say, *Dave, wait! I'm not going to Lemoine! Let me come with you!* But I don't. As I get in the car I think about what Mr. Marsh said, about how sometimes you just have to try to work things out with someone, just so you won't be wondering what would have happened.

The miles of road unroll in front of us. Josh and Doretha ride in the front seat, talking away, and I'm in the back, silent and moody. The tall stands of pine trees thin out and the land grows flatter and browner, and soon we're driving through mile after mile of prairie farmland. It's almost dark when we reach Lemoine.

When we arrive at the dorm, I remember that I haven't even asked Shantelle if I can stay in her room over the weekend. I'm not even positive she's back in the dorm. Jackie said something about how she was going to stay with some relative off campus in Lemoine, but that then she had moved back into the dorm. She's not even a real close friend of mine. Here I am showing up at 9:30 at night in her room, and I can only hope she'll be happy to see me.

The desk monitor tells me the number of the room Shan's staying in for the summer, which means at least she's in the dorm, and I go there and knock. After a minute, she answers.

"Alex! Hi!" she says, a little uncertainly.

"Hi, Shan. Listen, I'm back for the weekend. Is there any chance I can sleep on your floor or something?"

"Oh, no problem. You don't need to sleep on the floor. I haven't got a roommate, so you can stay in the extra bed."

Once I'm settled and Shan's lying down on her bed reading a romance novel, I feel really awkward. Like I said, we really don't hang around with each other much anymore, and it's not like I can suddenly start spilling my guts to her about the whole Mike McConnell thing. I'm sure she knows a lot more than I do about what Mike's up to this summer. I don't want to make myself look like an idiot, having come all the way down here to see him, if he's going out with someone else. And now that I think about it, he's almost certain to be dating someone else. Mike is never between girlfriends for very long. The more I think about it, the more stupid I feel for coming down here.

"So, how's Gary?" I ask. Gary's her boyfriend.

"He's all right," she says. "He's living off campus again this summer."

"I thought you were too."

"I was staying with my cousin for a while, but it didn't work out." Shantelle's not very talkative. I have to keep the conversation going if I'm ever going to find out anything.

"So, see anything of Tammy and those guys?"

Shantelle yawns, putting her book on the floor and rolling over on the bed. "Yeah, I see her some. She's sharing an apartment with Crystal Delacini. I don't think she's coming back here next year. They're pretty much partying all the time over there."

"Oh yeah? Any other PVA people hang out there, or is it mostly village people?"

Reaching up, Shantelle switches off her lamp. "There's a few. Walt doesn't hang out with them much anymore. Jackie's up at camp, of course, and Evan Slater's not here this summer. . . . Oh, Mike McConnell's around there sometimes, when he's not off being a big shot somewhere else."

I know what she means. Mike, unlike most people at PVA, refuses to stick with any one crowd. That's because he's so popular and gorgeous that girls in every group want to be with him, and since he's friendly and good at sports, the guys don't mind him either. He hangs around with rebels and dropouts like Tammy and her gang and their friends in Lemoine, but he's also welcome with some of the richest, snobbiest kids in school—the ones who are in good with all the teachers even though they can be pretty wild. And as for the more middle-of-the-road good kids, like the friends I've been hanging around with this year, he's popular with them too, especially since we all went on the mission trip to Santa Liana. But the important thing to me, right now, is that he still pals around with Tammy and Shantelle and Gary, so there's a way of me seeing him and getting in touch with him this weekend.

Shantelle's quiet so long I think she must have fallen asleep, so I get up and start getting ready for bed too. Then she says suddenly, "You're not still hung up on him, are you?" Which surprises me, because Shan's not normally all that nosy.

I don't answer right away, which I should realize is a dead giveaway. After a minute she says, "I thought you were dating someone up at camp."

"I was. I am. I don't know. No, I don't still like Mike." A pause as I get into bed. "Is he going out with anyone now?"

Shantelle laughs, like she knows I'm not going to be asking this question if I'm not still interested in him. "Nobody special. He's been hanging around Monika Dexter and her crowd a lot. I think he sort of had a thing going with her, but I'm not sure. And there's this girl in Lemoine—she goes to Regional I

72

think—and she's a friend of Tammy's. What's her name—Rochelle, that's it. Anyway she's got a big crush on Mike."

Switching off my light, I don't say anything more. After a while I think Shan really is asleep, from the way she's breathing. But I'm not. Not for a long, long time.

Next morning it's just like being back at school. Breakfast in the cafe, Sabbath school, church . . . I've been so used to spending Sabbath mornings up at camp, worshiping out in the campfire bowl or by the lake, surrounded by trees and water and sky, that it feels like something's missing when I'm inside. Shantelle has a little bottle of polish in her purse and does her nails during church. I'm amazed someone doesn't tell her to stop because the smell is not the kind of thing you could ignore. But academy church in summer is not as crowded as during school, so there aren't a lot of people around to be bothered.

After church we go to the cafe for lunch. As we leave and are hanging around on the steps, Shan's boyfriend Gary shows up, walking down from the parking lot. He nods at me.

"Hi, Alex. You finished at camp?"

"No, just down for the weekend."

"A bunch of us are going to the beach for the afternoon," Gary says. "You wanna go, Shan?"

"Sure, I guess."

"You wanna come too, Alex?"

"OK." I don't want to admit that my heart is pounding at the thought of who "a bunch of us" might include. Even if Mike's not there, there's a chance we could run into him-somewhere, somehow, sometime during the day. If I don't run into him sooner or later, the weekend will be over before I know it, and it will have been a wasted trip.

But I'm in luck. When Shantelle returns from signing out of the dorm for the afternoon, we head over to the parking lot, and there, hanging around a battered red car, are a bunch of kids. It's easy to pick out Tammy, sitting on the roof of the car in the shortest jean cutoffs you can imagine and a red tank top. There's another girl I don't recognize and a guy who looks kind of familiar, but it's the one leaning against the driver's door, jingling the keys in his hand, who I can't mistake. It's Mike. And it's time to find out if there was any point in me coming back here this weekend at all.

CHAPTER

8

Pile in, there's room for more!" Mike yells as we squeeze into his car in the parking lot. He's holding the door open, grinning like a maniac. I can see that his car is the biggest thing in his life. It's funny how guys are about their cars. The car is a dusty, beat-up red hatchback, about seven or eight years old, I think, with a bad paint job and a huge dent in the fender, but in Mike's mind it's a shiny new red sportscar and he's the coolest guy in the world driving it.

I'm about to crawl into the back seat with the others, but Mike says, "No, you get up front, Alex. You're the visitor." When he first saw me with Gary and Shan, I could tell he was shocked. What I couldn't tell was whether it was a good shock or a bad one.

This is going better than I ever dreamed. The backseat is already crowded. Gary's there with Shantelle on his lap, and the other guy—who turns out to be Kevin, who lives in Lemoine and attends Regional High—has Tammy on his lap. The girl I've never seen before must be Rochelle, the one who's supposed to have the crush on Mike. But she's not sitting in the front—I am.

When I'm in, Mike slides in and closes the door. He turns the key in the ignition and at first it sounds like nothing's going to happen, but after a few moans and grumbles the car gets started. A blast of solid sound hits my ears. Another thing about all these beat-up old cars guys drive, it always seems like the stereo system is worth more than the car. As if they don't care whether they're driving around a piece of junk as long as they can hear the music loud. Probably loud enough to cover the noise of the muffler falling off.

We pull away from the campus and head down the road into Lemoine. Tammy's voice shrieks from the back seat, singing along with the heavy metal music on the stereo. It's a hot day and of course the car isn't air-conditioned. The open windows just blow in heavy gusts of hot air. Mike is looking at the road, not at me. Last summer, when I first came to PVA, I would have found this so exciting—going to the beach on Sabbath afternoon with a bunch of "bad" kids, listening to rock music and everything. Now—I don't know, it's just not that exciting. Like I know these people's lives and they're really not that thrilling. Still, I'm glad to be here with Mike, even though I now find doing all this stuff on Sabbath makes me a little uncomfortable.

The ride doesn't last long. Lake Waganda, which is a tiny body of water surrounded by a very few, very scrubby trees, is just on the edge of Lemoine. The county park is here and there's a small beach and swimming area, which on a hot summer day like today is pretty crowded. Mike drives around the parking lot slowly, looking for cars that might belong to people he knows. They must be people from Lemoine, because I'm pretty sure no one else from PVA is here this afternoon.

Eventually he pulls into a parking spot and we all pile out. Finding a square of sand not already full of bodies, Tammy and the other girl—who really is Rochelle because that's what everyone's calling her—spread out a big blanket. Gary plunks down a tape player—which is going to sound really great since half the other people on the beach have stereos of some kind, all competing with each other—and

Mike pulls off his shirt to show off his gorgeous tanned body.

Probably the best thing about Mike—and there are lots of great things—is his build. He works out a lot and his muscles are really awesome. I can hardly take my eyes off him. Out of the corner of my eye I notice Rochelle is having the same problem.

But when Mike sits down on the blanket and takes a little bottle of sunscreen from Tammy, it's me, not Rochelle, he turns to. "Rub some of this on my back, will you, Alex?" he says. "I got a wicked burn on my shoulders a few weeks ago, and I don't want to do that again."

I start smoothing the cool liquid over his muscular shoulders. "Not as bad as the sunburns people were getting down in Santa Liana, I bet."

"No way!" Mike laughs. "Man, I thought my whole skin was going to peel off after the first day on the beach down there!"

"Where's that?" says Rochelle. She's kind of a short, stringy-looking girl with curly brown hair. Wearing a white tank top and red shorts, she appears really ticked off that Mike and I are getting along so well.

Mike hardly looks in her direction. "Santa Liana? Oh, it's just this place in the Caribbean where Alex and I were over spring break."

Alex and I? He makes it sound as if we took a little private vacation to our own little island paradise, and doesn't mention there were nearly 20 other kids and three teachers there, but who cares? Rochelle looks burned, which I'm sure is exactly what Mike intended.

"You want some on your back?" Mike asks. I peel off my T-shirt. Underneath is a bathing suit Shantelle loaned me when we went back to the dorm. It feels great to have Mike's strong hands putting the suntan lotion on me. I just can't believe we're together like this again.

Once the thrill of putting on the suntan lotion is over, the beach gets a little boring, though. Mike and Kevin and Gary go walking down the beach, looking for more girls to impress,

I guess. That leaves us four girls on the blanket—Tammy and Shan talking a little, Rochelle and I not saying anything at all. I think about Sabbath afternoons at camp. There's always so much planned, so much going on. Without meaning to, I picture Dave here. He wouldn't fit in with a crowd like this, that's for sure. I don't know if he'd put suntan lotion on my back. And he's definitely not as gorgeous as Mike. As Mike walks back across the sand, every girl on the beach watches him.

When he returns, he says, "Come on, Alex, let's go for a swim."

Rolling over, I glance at the swimming area, full of noisy screaming little kids. "Nah, it's all just little brats," I say. Last summer I'd have gone for a swim with Mike even if the water was full of hungry pirhanas. I guess I'm not quite that desperate any more. Then I realize it wouldn't be so bad to get alone with Mike, so I stroll down toward the water's edge with him. We walk along, ankle-deep in the water.

"So, you glad to get away from camp for the weekend?" he says.

"Yeah—I guess so. It's nice to have a weekend off, but I'm enjoying it."

Mike stretches, managing to flex several major muscle groups as he does it. Not that I'm complaining. "Yeah, well, camp's not for me," he says. "Too many rules—too much like school."

"If you feel that way about school, why *don't* you go to public school?" I know when I thought PVA's rules were way too strict—which I don't anymore, most of the time anyway—I didn't really have a choice about it. My parents were sending me there, and if they took me out it would only be to go to some worse academy or even home-schooling. They're like that. But from what Mike's said about his parents, who are divorced and both remarried, they don't really care what he does or where he goes. I can't really see what's keeping him at the Peeve if he doesn't want to be there.

"Might do that this school year. I really might," he says. Then his face quirks up into his cute, wicked grin. "But what would the deans and teachers do without me around? It'd be no fun without someone to give them a few headaches, would it?"

I smile back at him, and suddenly he reaches down and in one quick motion scoops up a handful of water and flicks it at my T-shirt. "Stop that!" I squeal, but it's too late and in seconds we're flinging water at each other, getting wetter and more giggly by the minute. And right in the middle of it, again not really meaning to, I remember Dave and our water fight last Thursday night on the campout. It's not like I'm thinking this is more fun or less fun than it was with Dave. It's just that he won't quite get out of my head.

Shaking my head as if I'm trying to clear it, I walk back toward the beach. Mike follows me. "What's wrong?" he asks. Just like Dave kept asking me what's wrong all those last couple weeks at camp. I can't believe it—me, Alex Best, stringing *two* guys along. Only I know I'm not really stringing Mike along. He can find someone else faster than he can flex his pecs. Rochelle's probably back there on the blanket waiting for him to rub sunscreen on *her* back right now.

But when we get back to the gang on the blanket, she's not there. Tammy grins up at Mike. "Rochelle went off with some guys from town," she says.

Mike shrugs, sitting down on the warm sand. "That's her loss," he says, and lies back in the sun.

I do the same, trying to let the sun pour down on my body and wipe out any confusion I feel. Isn't it enough just to be here on this lovely warm day, surrounded by a gang of friends, relaxing with no responsibilities? And even if Tammy's friends aren't exactly "my" crowd anymore, nobody's making me feel left out. I'm having a pretty good time.

It does get boring after a while though, just lying in the sun, talking a little but not much, listening to music. My mind keeps drifting back to camp and wondering what everyone else is doing there. When Tammy says, "Come on, I'm starved. Let's go get something to eat," I'm more than happy to pile back into the car. This time Mike doesn't actually *say* I should get in the front, but I do anyway. He doesn't talk to me a whole lot as we drive away from the beach and up the highway, not back into Lemoine but up to Halton, where there's a MacDonalds.

Going into MacDonalds feels weird too, because it's still Sabbath afternoon. I don't feel like saying that to the crowd, because what would I do—sit out in the car or on the sidewalk while they eat? Wouldn't that give Mike and Tammy a laugh? I know they already think I've become all holy because this past school year I hung around with different friends and wasn't out getting into trouble with them anymore. And they're right, I have changed. For a while there when I first came to PVA last summer, I was so happy to get away from home that I didn't care about whether things were right or wrong. But since Santa Liana, I've gotten to know God a little bit for myself, and now I feel different. I don't like the thought that I'm letting Him down—and that's *definitely* what it seems to me that I'm doing, sitting there in MacDonald's while everyone munches their Big Macs or slurps their milkshakes. I don't have any money so there's no real issue about whether I should spend it on Sabbath; but Mike offers to buy me something, so I take a chocolate shake from him and then wonder if I should be guilty about *that*. Is it guilt I feel, or just being out of place?

After the fast food we drive back to Lemoine in time to drop Shan off on campus; since she's living in the dorm she has to make it to sundown worship. I noticed last summer, and it's still true, that Shan has a flair for living close to the edge but just inside the rules—a talent that none of the rest of Tammy's gang shares. She does pretty much all the same things they do, but she almost never gets in trouble. Partly it's because she's so quiet, I think, but she also does things like getting back in time for worship, and bothering to go to the dean for a late pass afterward.

I figure there's no real need for me to get to worship, so I stay in the car with Mike, Tammy, and Kevin. Gary stayed back on campus with Shantelle, though they've promised to catch up with us later.

"Where to now?" Mike asks, looking back at Tammy. It's something her friends always do whenever she's around—look at her like she's the boss, the woman with all the answers.

"Let's go to my place," she says. As she does I can tell she loves saying "my place" just as much as Mike loves saying "my car." She's only 17—a year older than me—and she's living totally independently, this summer at least, staying in an apartment with Crystal Delacini. Crystal's a few years older than us, and she has an apartment that she usually shares with another girl, Sheri, only Sheri's away for the summer. Their apartment's a major hangout in Lemoine, especially for certain PVA dorm kids when they can get off campus. I'm sure Tammy just delights in living at Party Central. When I think about the difference between Tammy's family and mine—I'm lucky they will even let me cross the street alone—my mind just spins. Do her parents even care that she's sharing an apartment with a girl who thinks classy entertaining is when you have glasses for people to drink their beer from?

Soon we're once again pulling up in front of the ramshackle old house in which Crystal rents an apartment. It's too hot to go inside so we head for the backyard, where I'm not surprised to see not only Crystal but about six other people, none of whom I know, sitting around on the grass. And this is where the weirdness particularly starts—the part of the weekend that *really* makes me see how big the gap is between what I left behind at camp and what I've found here in Lemoine. Just like I'd expect, they're all drinking beer. Two or three of them are smoking. As soon as we sit down, Tammy lights up a cigarette and Mike and Kevin each crack open a beer.

As Tammy takes a long draw on her smoke she looks over at me with half-closed eyes, like she's daring me to say something or react. I hate it when people do that, showing off how "bad" they are, how tough. Although I guess I've done a bit of it myself. Anyway, if it's supposed to make me feel like I'm stupid for not smoking, it totally doesn't work on me because I think the habit is the grossest thing on earth. Drinking,

I can sort of understand. I tried it once and it didn't really do much for me. I think people act really stupid and gross while they're drunk, but at least I can *understand* why someone might want to get drunk and forget whatever was bothering them, or act like they're part of the crowd. Smoking—well, that's just beyond me. But Tammy obviously thinks it makes her look cool.

The whole atmosphere of the place is uncomfortable to me, and to make matters worse, Mike basically ignores me. He was so cozy and friendly at the beach, but since then he's been hardly talking to me at all. I run back over the afternoon in my mind, wondering if I've said or done anything to make him mad. I did kind of walk away from him at one point on the beach, but I didn't think I really cut him off or anything. Just this afternoon I thought everything was perfect and he was interested again, but now it's hard to tell.

For the first time all day I admit to myself that I really wish I was back at camp. Somehow, I just feel more at home there. And if Mike's not paying any special attention to me, then there's really nothing keeping me here.

After we've been sitting around the yard for about an hour, the sky starts to cloud over like it might be going to rain. "There's supposed to be a thunderstorm," Crystal announces, getting up and folding up her blanket. We all trail behind her into the house, which is hot and stuffy because the air conditioner's broken. Crystal opens a couple of bags of chips and somebody passes around a few more bottles of beer. I'm keeping an eye on Mike—I think he's had two or three to drink now. This is new to me. I mean, I always knew he was wild and tough and didn't mind drinking and stuff, but I've never really seen him do it. I can't quite decide how it makes me feel about him. He still isn't saying much to me.

Tammy flicks on the TV, and immediately they're all fascinated by some rock video. It's still a little while until sundown, and I really wish I wasn't here. Even though it's raining now, I go out onto the little balcony that Crystal has at the end of her upstairs room. There's barely room for two people out there, but it's an OK place to sit, sheltered under the eaves, and watch the rain shaking the leaves and see the light slip away as evening comes on. I guess it's just the habit of sundown worship on Sabbath evening—at home, at school, at camp—that makes me suddenly want to pray. But there's not much I can say. I'm sure God doesn't approve of where I am and who I'm hanging out with today, so He probably doesn't want to hear from me.

But I find myself doing it all the same, putting my thoughts into words. "God, I'm really mixed up. I came back here to see if Mike still likes me and if I still like him. But I can't figure anything out. The only thing is, I know I don't belong with this crowd anymore. But I'm still not sure where I do belong. Can You give me some answers, God?"

But I hear only the splattering of rain, the distant rumble of thunder, an occasional flash of lightning, and the sound of a car engine pulling up below. The voices spilling out of the car tell me Gary and Shantelle are here, and some other people too, it sounds like. Another car arrives, doors slam, more voices. Sounds like it's turning into a real party.

The door behind me opens, and I look up startled, not sure who it is I expect to see. But it's Mike. And I'm frozen for a second, wondering if this is the answer I asked for in my prayer.

It's obvious from the expression on his face he's not surprised to see me here. He knew I was out here, and he came out looking for me. And he can't—he *can't*—have forgotten that it was on this very same balcony, another Saturday night, another one of Crystal's parties, that he kissed me for the very first time last summer.

"Hiding out?" he says, sinking down to sit on the rough boards of the balcony beside me.

"A little, I guess."

"Well, I won't let you hide away forever. I had to come find you."

And what's *that* supposed to mean? Now that he's so close, I can smell the sharp tang of beer on his breath, but he's not acting drunk or anything. It's hard to tell if he's behaving any differently because of the beer, or because of—something else.

"Well, you found me." Oooh, lame answer there, Alex.

"I've found you, and I don't want to lose you again," Mike says. "I've missed you, Alex. We had a good time together last summer, didn't we?"

I nod, finding suddenly that I can't say anything. Whatever the spell was that he used to cast over me, it's still there. It's a spell of— excitement, I guess, and danger. And I like that. With a guy like Dave, things would never be dangerous. And I don't know if I want my whole life to be safe and predictable. Mike's like the hero of some romance novel. Tall, dark, and handsome, and you never know what he's going to do next.

What he does do next is to lean forward and kiss me. And I can even ignore the beer on his breath when his lips touch mine and every nerve in my body begins jumping. After that, neither of us says anything much for a while.

When we do take a break, Mike says, "Want to go back inside? Everyone's talking about driving up to Halton to see a late movie or something."

I don't want to—going to a movie, that is, going with a crowd of people. We'll have no time to talk, and tomorrow I have to leave. I need time alone with Mike. But when I don't answer right away, he says, "Come on, it'll be fun. Have a bit of a laugh before you have to head back to camp."

Standing, he holds out his hand to help me up and takes me back into Crystal's living room, still holding tightly to my hand. Holding his hand feels wonderful. A lot more people are in the room now than when I went outside. Tammy and Kevin are still there, and Gary and Shan, and a few more kids I don't recognize, and one I do—Rochelle.

She's sitting on the arm of the couch, and the minute Mike and I enter her eyes focus on us like searchlights. If looks could kill I'd drop dead from the glare she shoots me as she sees me and Mike holding hands. Mike just gives this little grin, looks away, and squeezes my hand.

And suddenly it all falls into place for me. There in that

crowded, smoky room with the pounding music and everyone talking and laughing, I can see Mike McConnell's game totally. He was all over me today at the beach as long as Rochelle was there. When she left, he ignored me. But when she came back, he went out on the balcony and got me. For that one second it's blindingly clear to me that he's using me to make her jealous. And for all I know, somewhere else in town he's been playing Rochelle against some other girl because it is all just a big game to him—the game he's so good at.

My head reels as I think this through, in a split second of understanding, and I realize Mike's still holding my hand as he tows me down the stairs toward the front door. Other people are getting up too. The three cars out on the street—Mike's and two others—fill up with Crystal's partygoers, heading out to Halton. Mike has a beer in his hand again, one he picked up while walking through the living room, and every commercial I've ever heard about drinking and driving flashes through my head as he opens the door to his car. I want to say, *Mike, don't! Should you be driving?* But he'd be mad if I even suggested anything like that. What can I do? Walk away? Go back to the dorm? But Mike says, "Get in the front, Alex," and moving like I'm in a dream, I do.

Tammy and Kevin slide in behind us, and Rochelle stalks past, making it real obvious she's not even looking at Mike, to climb in the back of the same car Gary and Shantelle are in. I'm not sure who the guy is who's driving. Most of the rest of the crowd are not PVA people. I don't know any of the kids in the third car. But Mike guns his engine and peels away, in the lead, driving way too fast for the quiet streets of Lemoine.

It's dark out by now and rain is still beating against the windshield, keeping the wipers working at full speed. The radio is pounding. My stomach tightens into a knot as Mike pulls out to pass another car. It isn't a divided highway, and the headlights of another car shoot up out of nowhere in the lane we're in. Mike pulls back just in time, cursing under his breath. "Don't you think you should slow down a little?" I manage to gasp.

"What? Scared, are you?" Mike glances at me out of the corner of his eye and laughs. Then he looks back over his shoulder, not even keeping his eyes on the dark, wet road. "Kevin, Alex is scared! She thinks I'm drivin' too fast! What do ya think I should do?"

Kevin laughs. "Give it to 'er!" he says, and Mike pulls out to pass again, although we're on a double line this time, and floors the pedal. The car jerks ahead, but the car in the other lane doesn't pull back. I glance over to see that that car, too, is loaded with teenagers. I don't think it's one of those that left Crystal's place with us. I think they're all behind us. But it doesn't matter. Whether he knows these guys or not, Mike is apparently convinced he has to drag-race with them.

We're speeding along, both cars side by side on a two-lane highway, Mike giving the car all he's got, the wipers pumping away furiously. From the back seat Kevin and Tammy both yell "Come on! You can take him!" Then it happens again, but much too quickly this time. Headlights. High up, like the headlights of a truck. They must have come around a curve. I barely see them before Mike slams the brake. The car skids on the wet pavement. A horn blows, the other car's brakes squeal, and then we swerve wildly to the side and there's a sickening crunch and a jolt. Someone's screaming. My body flies forward and stops, pinned by the seatbelt, and the headlights flash closer and closer and swerve away. Another crunch, seconds after the first, and I can still hear that voice screaming. Then everything is quiet.

CHAPTER

9

The moments after the accident are a jumble of confusion. I must be in shock or something, because the first thing I'm clearly aware of is someone opening the door of the car and trying to pull me outside. It takes me a second to register that my seatbelt's still holding me in the car. Unbuckling it, I stumble out into a nightmare scene.

Mike's car sits crosswise across the highway, its rear end crumpled. A few yards ahead is the car we were drag-racing with—the back and driver's side of that car are crushed, too. In the ditch on the other side of the road is a truck, a four-wheel drive, lying on its side. Other cars have already pulled up to stop. People swarm everywhere, but nobody seems familiar until I turn and see Mike, standing dazed beside his car. Blood trickles from his nose down his lip, but he doesn't seem to notice.

I should move, do something, say something. It's only then that I realize Tammy and Kevin are still in the back of Mike's car, and it's silent in there. People are trapped in the other car too, and I can hear voices shouting from the truck as well. And then, far off, I hear a siren—it sure doesn't take the cops long to get here—and up ahead I see red and blue lights reflecting off the shiny pavement. Mike swears. I realize he probably did have too much to drink, that he really was driving impaired, and he's probably in a whole lot of trouble now.

As the police car pulls to a stop, Mike looks over at me. "Look, Alex," he says, "if the cops ask you anything, don't tell them nothing, OK? Just don't get me in trouble." His eyes are fierce above his bloody nose, and I can't believe he didn't ask how I am or say a word about Tammy or Kevin or the people in the other cars—just about me not getting him in trouble.

Everything blurs again, and I'm not sure exactly what happens, although I know an ambulance arrives—maybe two. Guys get out of an ambulance with stretchers and start taking Tammy and Kevin out of the car. The police are talking to Mike and the other drivers. I hear Mike arguing back with one of the policemen, his voice rising to an angry shout, and I wonder just how stupid he can be. Then a woman police officer stands in front of me with a little notebook and a pen.

"Are you hurt?" she asks.

"Um, no— I don't— I'm not sure."

"What's your name?"

"Alex Best. Um, my full name is Julia Alexandra Best."

"OK, Alex, and were you a passenger in this car?" She nods at the sad-looking heap of Mike's precious red car.

I nod, feeling suddenly woozy and sick. Then I remember what Mike said to me and enough anger flares up in me to clear my head for a second. Out of the corner of my eye I see them placing Tammy on a stretcher. She looks as white as the sheet she's lying on.

"Listen, officer," I say as clearly as I can manage through the sudden pain in my head, "if you have any questions, if you want to know anything about what happened, I'll be glad to tell you. I can give you my phone number— I'm working at camp this summer, but I was down here for the weekend . . . "

She nods thoughtfully and copies down the dorm and

camp phone numbers as I give them to her. "We may call you if we need any information," she says.

"Like I said, I'll be happy to give it." I remember Mike grinning and pushing down on the gas when I told him to slow down. I guess the way I say that makes the officer listen, because she says, "Was your friend drinking when he was driving the car?"

"Well, yes, he was drinking earlier," I say. "And I'm pretty sure he was driving over the speed limit too." Tammy is being lifted into the ambulance. Suddenly I blurt out, "I want to go to the hospital."

"Do you think you're hurt?" the policewoman asks again.

"I—I don't know. I feel weird. But I want to go with Tammy. I have to see if she's OK." I don't think I'm making much sense, but the officer leads me over to the ambulance, where the paramedics load me on next to Tammy's stretcher. It looks like she's unconscious. I remember Mike mentioning the back seat had no seatbelts and Tammy and Kevin laughing like they'd never use them anyway. The siren of the ambulance, as it pulls away, seems to fill my whole head.

At the Lemoine County Hospital emergency room our arrival is the big news of the night. The admitting nurse takes one quick glance at me and tells me to go sit down, which I figure means there's nothing really wrong with me. Everyone's attention has already focused on the stretchers as the medical technicians wheel in Tammy, Kevin, one girl from the other car, and a man from the truck. Unable to see Tammy clearly, I still don't even know if she's dead or alive. Everything's spinning around me. I don't know where Mike is. Sitting down, I put my head between my knees, and eventually the sick, faint feeling passes and I find myself alone in a strange emergency room.

Nobody is in the waiting room except an older man with his arm in a sling and a woman with a crying baby who never seems to settle down. The TV blares nonsense that I can't focus on. Suddenly I remember quite clearly what I can't recall noticing before—that as I climbed up into the ambulance, the police

89

were leading Mike to a police car. *Will they bring him here to the hospital,* I wonder, *or straight to the police station?* He didn't look like he was badly hurt, though he must have hit his face on the steering wheel to get that nosebleed. I don't remember hitting anything at all, just being jolted around.

From the way Mike was yelling at them, the police must have wanted him to take a breathalyzer test or something. He's in big trouble this time for sure. And instead of keeping my mouth shut and bailing him out like he wanted, I told the police everything I knew. And I'd tell them more if I got a chance.

Which doesn't make me feel any better about things.

After what seems like a long, long time a nurse comes out and calls my name, and I go in past the office to a little curtained-off cubicle where some guy—I don't know if he's a nurse or a doctor or a med student or what—enters with a clipboard and asks me a bunch of questions about the accident, shines a light in my eyes, tells me to move my head a bunch of different ways, and inquires if anything hurts. "I just think you're a little bit in shock," he says, "but you don't seem to have been injured. You're very lucky."

"I know. What about the— the others— Tammy, how is she?"

When he frowns, I realize he's not about to tell me one thing. "They're examining her. We don't really know the extent of her injuries yet." His eyes shift away from me, then back with a fake cheerful expression. "As for you, Miss Best, I think the best thing you could do is go home and get a good night's rest, all right?"

"All right."

It's when I walk back into the waiting room that I realize that I have no one to take me to the dorm, no way of getting back. I don't know what happened to Gary and Shantelle. They never did show up at the hospital. Since they weren't in the accident, they probably didn't want to get involved. And there's really no one back at the dorm I can call to come get me. Only Shan, who has already deserted me, or over at the guys' dorm, Walt, who doesn't have a car or any way of getting out here.

90

I don't have the money for a taxi or anything, and it's after 11:00. I don't know how far it is from the hospital to the campus but it's too far to walk—especially the way I'm feeling now. Suddenly I feel more alone than I've ever felt in my life. I'd give anything, *anything* to have one of my good friends here now—even Walt, who I hardly said hi to in church this morning, or one of my girlfriends like Dana or Heather or Stacey—or Dave. And with that thought I feel suddenly relieved, as if Dave is the person who could make this all right, take care of me, get me home safely. Of course he's hundreds of miles away, doesn't know where I am, and probably wouldn't be too impressed with me if he *did* know, but Dave's the one I want here now.

And as I sit there in the emergency room, hardly even aware that tears are rolling slowly down my cheeks, I realize what a stupid waste of time this whole weekend has been. Whatever Mr. Marsh said about having to take a chance and go back to find out if it would have worked, this wasn't worth it. No matter what was going on, Dave would never leave me scared and alone in a hospital emergency room with no way of getting home. If Dave was driving too fast and I wanted him to slow down, he wouldn't drive like a maniac just because he got a thrill out of scaring me. And, of course, he wouldn't be drinking and driving in the first place because he's not a complete idiot like someone I could mention—someone who only wants to have me around if he can use me to make another girl feel lousy!

Without realizing it I've gone in two minutes from feeling lonely and desolate to outraged and furious. My hands have clenched into fists, and if Mike McConnell hadn't already gone off with the police, I'd be more than happy to throw him in the lockup myself, with maybe a good old-fashioned punishment like a whipping to remind him what a jerk he is.

"Alex? You still here?"

"What?" Snapping out of my happy fantasy of torturing Mike, I see Shantelle standing there, looking nervous and uncomfortable.

"When I reached the dorm I realized you probably didn't have any way back, and I didn't know if you were OK or anything, so I got Gary to bring me back. We got permission, but I've got to be right back. Do you want to come back to the dorm?"

"Yes!" I stand up, so glad to see her and so eager to get out of this nightmare place.

"How—how's Tammy?" Shantelle asks. "Was she hurt bad?"

I don't even want to think about Tammy, her face all white and blood on her forehead. "I—I don't know, Shan. They've still got her in there. Nobody's told me anything. We'll have to find out later."

As I sit in the back of the car neither Shan nor Gary has much to say on the way to PVA. Which is fine with me because I've got a lot of thinking to do. And it doesn't even all get straightened out until much later, when I'm lying sleepless in the bed in Shantelle's room, running over and over the events of that day and night. It seems like it's been much longer than one day since I woke up in this room this morning. I've gone through so many ups and downs, such a roller-coaster of feelings.

The past few hours since the accident are hard to remember. I realize that, as the doctor said, I've been in shock, and that's why it's taken a while for it to sink in about Tammy—how badly hurt she is and how worried I am about her. She isn't really my friend anymore, but I sure don't want her to die or be like a vegetable or anything. Nobody deserves that—not even Mike, though he deserved to get hurt if anyone does. And all he got was a bloody nose!

I'm still mad at Mike, my insides boiling and churning, but after a while I realize not everything that happened today was his fault. I mean, yeah, he really did use me to get at Rochelle—I'm sure of that. And he really did drink and drive and show off, which is way worse. But as for *me*, Julia Alexandra Best, I didn't have to go along with any of that. Nobody forced me to get in that car with him, or to kiss him out on the balcony, or even to come back here this weekend to see him in the first place. That was all my idea. And if I came hoping to figure things out, well, I've figured them out.

I love PVA, even though I complain about it like everyone does, but I'm sure glad to see it fading in the distance behind me the next morning as Josh and Doretha drive me away from campus. Gossip's already gotten around town about the car accident—Doretha's family lives in Lemoine—and when they hear I was one of the kids in it, of course they want to know all about it. Up to the time we left campus no one had any news about how Tammy was, and I don't know how much trouble Mike's in or anything, so I'm still left not knowing much, and I'm really not all that thrilled to talk about it. Fortunately they understand and after a while they stop pressing me for details. It feels so great to be headed back to camp. I guess what I really love about PVA is my friends and, with most of them up at camp now, camp is where I want to be.

Oh, I did see one friend before I left PVA. Walt came over to the dorm to say hi and goodbye. He was really worried when he heard about the accident, which I guess is only normal. Hugging me, he told me he was glad I was OK. He really is kind of a sweetheart. And amazingly, he really does have a girlfriend this summer—some little freshman girl, which is nice for him—so it does look like we can be just friends after all. I hope it lasts because I wouldn't want to lose him as a friend. I don't know if I can really count Shantelle as a close friend anymore, although it was nice of her to return for me last night. But that whole gang—Tammy's gang—I just don't think I'll be seeing much of them at all this school year.

And, of course, that includes Mike McConnell. For sure this time.

The hours slip away, and soon we're within sight of camp. As we drive up the road to it I think about getting back to work in the kitchen, about everyone wanting to know all about the accident as soon as they hear about it. But mostly, I have to admit, I'm thinking about Dave. One thing that never really occurred to me when I went flying off to PVA on Friday was what would happen if things *didn't* work out with me and Mike. Maybe Dave wasn't planning to just wait around forever till I made up my mind. If he's gotten sick of waiting, I wouldn't blame him.

As we pull into the parking lot, the place looks pretty quiet. A few cars arrive with kids for the next week's camp, but I don't see any staff members around until we've unpacked the car and I'm heading over to Cabin 14, my knapsack slung over my shoulder. That's when I spot him. Dave, walking away from me across the campgrounds, hands in his pockets, heading toward the lake, not even noticing me.

I'm so happy to see him I just want to race over and give him a huge hug, but considering the way we were both feeling when I left, maybe it's better if I don't. Maybe it would be better if I just wait till later, let some time go by . . .

But I've already tried that with friendships. It doesn't work. They don't get better if you leave them alone—they just get harder to fix. "Hey, Dave!" I call out.

Stopping, he turns slowly and looks back. Although he doesn't come over to me, he doesn't walk away either. He just says, "Hi, Alex," and stands there waiting.

Which means, unless I just ignore him and head for the cabin, I have to do all the work. I have to go to him. But considering that I was the one who couldn't make up my mind, maybe that's OK. I start across what suddenly seems like the longest stretch of grass in the country, hoping and praying I haven't thrown away a great friendship—and maybe more—on a guy who wasn't worth it.

When I get right up in front of Dave, he's still not smiling—just looking. Not like he's mad or anything but just standing there. It's actually kind of unnerving.

"How was your weekend?" I said. "Did you go home?"

A shake of his head. "Nah, I decided to stay up here after all. It wasn't bad." Then, after a short pause, "How was yours?"

"Umm—" I hesitate for a second over what to tell him, and decide on the truth. "Lousy!"

94

Dave almost smiles at my outburst. "Was it really that bad?"

"Well, I was bored to death, I didn't like hanging around *any* of my old friends anymore, I almost got killed by a drunk driver in a car accident, and I missed you like crazy. Other than that it was OK."

Although I was hoping to make him laugh, what I get is even better. His eyes widen in shock. "Are you *serious?* You were in a car accident? Was it a bad one? Were you hurt at all?"

I almost stumble over myself, too eager to explain that no, really, I'm fine, everything's OK. But he's just like I thought of him being when I was in the emergency room last night. Forgetting our stupid fight and everything, all he cares about is whether I'm OK. Exactly the opposite of Mike who couldn't think about anything but whether I would rat on him or not. Dave, the guy I practially dumped, is totally focused on how I am and whether I was hurt. What can you say about a guy like that?

And that's where I could leave things, and where I almost do. Dave doesn't ask any questions about Mike McConnell— in fact, once he's sure I wasn't hurt in the accident, he doesn't question me about the weekend at all. Instead he carries my stuff down to the cabin and then we go in to supper, and I sit with all my friends and tell them the whole story about the accident. Jackie, of course, wants to know if Tammy's OK, so after supper she and I hunt Mrs. Edwards, who by now has heard the whole accident story from other people. I guess a car accident involving a possibly drunk driver when the driver and some passengers are PVA students is pretty big news in our little world. Mrs. Edwards promises us that later tonight she'll phone Mrs. Reichman at the PVA dorm and find out what the news is on Tammy.

"That's wild," Jackie says as we walk back to the cabin after talking to Mrs. Edwards. "I mean, it's just what you'd expect from someone like Mike. He's always trying to show off how tough and how cool he is. Sorry, I hope you're still not—you know—thinking about him and stuff."

"After this weekend? Definitely not!" I assure her.

Jackie shakes her head. "And Tammy's the kind who'd go right along with it," she says. "Except for Mike himself, I don't think there's anyone worse she could be going out with than that Kevin guy. He's nothing but trouble. I wish Tammy would smarten up and get a life." Then she laughs her short, sarcastic laugh. "Listen to me! Don't I sound like *I've* got it all together."

"No, I understand," I say quickly. "Tammy's your friend. I can see why you'd be worried about her."

I'm brushing my hair in front of the tiny mirror in our cabin, getting ready to go down to campfire. Someone knocks on the door. "Just a minute," I say as Jackie finshes putting on her jeans. When I open the door, Dave's standing there.

"You ready to go down to campfire?" he asks.

At campfire he and I sit together on a back bench far away from the platform and from everybody else. Some of the older staff guys have formed a quartet and they're doing sort of a mini-concert as part of the campfire program. While they're harmonizing and the fire's crackling away, Dave turns to me and whispers, "I missed you, too, this weekend."

I nod. "I shouldn't have gone. It was a dumb idea."

"I wish you hadn't. I thought—I figured you were going back to see that other guy, the one you liked down there."

This is where I could just drop the whole thing, pretend Mike McConnell never happened. But if there's one thing that's been cool about my whole friendship with Dave, it's that it hasn't been full of playing stupid games like most guy-girl friendships are. And after seeing the kind of games Mike played this weekend, pitting one girl against another, I just want more than anything to be really honest and straightforward.

"It was, kind of," I say softly, and immediately wish I hadn't because he does look hurt. Well, of course he would. But I plow on anyway. "I couldn't get this guy out of my mind—especially after he wrote me and then showed up here at family camp—so I wanted to go back and see if there was anything between us. I shouldn't have gone. It was a stupid waste of time."

Dave still looks hurt. "He wasn't interested, huh?"

"No, *I* wasn't interested!" I whisper back. "He was, kind of—in his own way. But it's not a way I'm interested in. And I knew that even *before* he almost got us all killed with his crazy driving."

"*He* was the one who did that?" Dave asks in surprise.

"Yeah, but don't worry, I won't be going driving with him again."

We quiet down then, to listen to the music, but after staff meeting that night Dave asks me to go for a quick walk before lights out. "I need to tell you something, Alex," he says.

"What?"

"Well, I was really mad at you this weekend. When you went away. But when you came back today, and then when you told me about the accident, I was so worried about you. The thing is, Alex, I still mean what I said the night we went on the campout. About you and me. I do want us to go on being friends, and I'd like to be more than friends. Especially if it works out for me to go to PVA this year."

I want to answer, but for a minute I can't. I think I might almost start to cry, which would be too weird for words, but I get it under control and say, "That's what I—I'd like that too, Dave. I mean—this whole thing this weekend, it really made me see that what we've got is cool. It's what I want. What I mean is, in a way this weekend was all about me making a choice between two guys—you and Mike. I'm sorry, but I had to figure that out for myself because after the way he treated me last year, I guess I still felt like I was worthless if I couldn't get him back. But I learned a lot this weekend, and not just that I like you better than Mike."

"If that's all you learned, it'd be OK by me," Dave says. I smile and squeeze his hand. "But the thing is, it was like a choice between two ways of life. Last summer I thought it would be cool to hang out with the tough crowd, drink and drive fast and all that. Then over the school year I met a different crowd and I started learning about God and being a Christian. And this weekend I found out—I don't want to go back. If the other kind of life has all the thrills, that's too bad. I don't want those kind of thrills."

That's quite a serious speech for me, but there's something about Dave that makes me feel safe saying those kinds of things. He takes me seriously. "I'm glad you made that decision, Alex," he says. "Because I don't want that kind of life either. I'm a Christian, and I'm always going to be one, and I was hoping we could share that."

By now he's holding both my hands, and I squeeze them both. "We can," I say as he leans forward for a good-night kiss.

CHAPTER

10

The last few weeks of camp just whiz by. The news from Lemoine is interesting—Tammy's doing better, but she was pretty badly injured in the accident, some broken bones and stuff, so she's gone back up to Wilcox, where her family is, to recuperate. And Mike's back with his parents in Wilcox too, after being charged with impaired driving causing bodily harm or something like that. He won't be driving for a while since he doesn't have his license anymore; and he won't be doing much of anything except working to pay off his fine, it looks like. And it also appears that neither Mike nor Tammy will be at PVA for the coming school year. Mike just may get his wish about going to public school after all.

I can't say I'll miss either of them much. This summer has really made me appreciate the friends I have—the ones up here, especially. I've gotten really close to almost all the other PVA kids on staff, even though back at school we all hang out with different cliques. And of course there's one non-PVA person I've become very close to also. Dave and I spend lots of time together, getting along better than ever, and I have to admit that Mike McConnell doesn't cross my mind very much these days at all.

Finally it's the last week of camp. The campers are all gone, leaving just us staff doing cleanup and chores and basically closing things down for the year; and also relaxing and getting to spend some time together without all the pressures we have all summer long. Late on Thursday afternoon I'm sprawled on the grass down near the lake, putting the finishing touches on the tan I've been carefully working on all summer. When you're as redheaded as I am, you really have to concentrate on not burning to a crisp. Heather, Lacey, and Jackie are all lying nearby, enjoying a few minutes of sun before we have to go back and do some actual work.

"I can't believe we're really leaving here on Sunday," Heather says. "I mean, it seems like just yesterday we got here."

"Not for me," Jackie replies. "Seems like the summer's gone on forever. I can hardly even remember what school looks like!"

"I *wish* I couldn't remember," Lacey comments.

I know what Jackie means, though. In one way it's like it's all gone by so quickly, but in another way, so much has happened in the eight weeks we've spent up here at Camp Westhaven that it seems impossible one summer could have held it all.

"Well, better get used to the idea of school," Heather says, "because when we get home from camp, there's just two more weeks, and it's back to the Peeve."

"Don't rush it!" Lacey says. "My mom and dad are taking us camping before school starts."

"Oooh, more camping—just what you need," I laugh.

"Yeah, but this is luxury camping," Lacey points out. "You oughta see our motor home!"

"I just can't wait to get home for two weeks of hot showers," Jackie sighs. "To me, that'll be all the luxury I need."

"What about you, Alex?" Heather asks. "What are you going to do with your two weeks of freedom?"

"Um—I'm not sure." Going back to Fairview for two

weeks isn't my idea of heaven, but I guess it won't be too boring if it's just for a couple weeks. "Dave asked me to come down and visit his family for a few days, but I doubt my parents will go for that."

"Why not?" Lacey asks. "I mean, you'd be with his *family*. It's not as if you'd be off with him alone somewhere."

"You've got to know my parents," I explain wearily. "They're just super-strict. They'd flip if they even knew I *had* a boyfriend, never mind wanting to go spend the weekend at his place."

"What a pain," Heather says. "I'm going to Trevor's place for a whole week before school, and my folks don't mind at all."

"Yeah, well, don't remind me," I say. Like I need to know how cool her parents are compared to mine.

Mine aren't as bad as they used to be, I'll admit. Since I went to PVA, and especially since the trip to Santa Liana, they've sort of accepted that I'm halfway to being an adult. Now I can go out and do things on my own sometimes. But they're still very conservative, and I know that even though I'm 16, they're not crazy about the idea of me dating anyone. In fact, I don't know *when* they *do* think is a good time to start dating. I believe my stepdad's ideal would be for me to have some kind of arranged marriage at about the age of 21. Well, news for you, Dad, it's not gonna happen that way. Though Dad's been a little easier to get along with since his illness back in the spring, that's like saying the ocean is a little bit drier—it doesn't really make a whole lot of difference.

Still, when Dave takes me out in the canoe later that day, he's so sure we're going to get to spend a few days together down at his place.

"It'll be great, Alex," he says enthusiastically. "There's so much stuff I want to show you. And I know my mom's going to love you."

"Well, I just hope it works out."

"Sure—like I hope it works out for me to go to PVA this year."

"Your folks still aren't sure."

"No, but they've been on the phone to the PVA business office every day, trying to figure out how they can work it out. I mean, they'd really like for me to go; they just don't see how they can afford it. Hey, want to go up on the island?"

We're canoeing past the island where we had our campout earlier in the summer. As we haul the canoe up on the beach, laughing about the water fight we had here that night, I remember something. "Dave, do you know *why* we had this campout in the first place?"

"Just to get away, I thought—why?"

"The whole thing was this big scheme Stacey'd cooked up. You see, she wanted to get Mr. Marsh together with Mrs. Krause; she's always thought they'd be the perfect couple. She figured if she asked them to chaperone our campout, they'd end up together!"

Dave laughs. "Well, Mr. Marsh left camp early, so who knows, maybe he went to visit Mrs. Krause. But Stacey's sure got nerve. I don't think I'd try to go matchmaking with any of my teachers!"

I sit down on the warm sand beside him. "Well, PVA's cool like that. I mean, you really do get to know the teachers like they're people. Of course, I feel that way about Mr. Marsh and the Edwards' especially because we went to Santa Liana together."

"Oh, yeah, that's another thing. If I can get to PVA this year I *definitely* want to join Action and go on the mission trip," Dave says. "Although, again, I don't know where the money would come from."

"You'd be surprised," I tell him. "I didn't think I could come up with it either, but I managed. My mom helped some, but—I really think God did a lot of it."

"God can do some amazing things," Dave agrees. "I'd just love to get into another country and see what it's like, do something useful for the people there." He starts scooping up the sand into a small sand castle. "I've finally decided that's what I'd really like to do with my life. I mean, something that involves working in the Third World, maybe with some international aid agency or something."

"That's cool," I agree. "Ever since I went to Santa Liana, I've made up my mind that whatever I do, I want it to involve lots of traveling. I've thought about being an airline stewardess, but I don't think that would be so good because I wouldn't be seeing different places. I mean, I'd be traveling around, but I wouldn't be staying there."

"No, that wouldn't be so great," Dave agrees. "I mean, not if you want to really spend some time in a place and find out what it's like. But I'd like to help people as well as just travel. Working in the Third World could be pretty dangerous, but exciting too."

"Dangerous?" I had never thought about it that way.

"Well, it depends where you go. But sometimes you can be in a place, thinking it's not dangerous, and then it can get really scary. My uncle's family were missionaries in Rwanda when the civil war started there a few years ago. You oughta hear my cousin tell about it. They were lucky to get out when they did. And some people *don't* leave. They stay in places, even when there's a war on, and work in refugee camps and stuff. I think I'd like that."

"Wow, I never thought about doing stuff like that. I mean, I always thought about being a missionary as just like being a teacher or a doctor or whatever, only in another country. But being in places where there was a war on and stuff— I'd be scared, but you're right, it *would* be exciting."

"My uncle says if there's one thing you learn, it's that you really have to trust God at a time like that," Dave continues. "I think it would be a terrific thing to do."

I nod. I can't even imagine what Mom and Dad would say about me going off to a war-torn country, but by that time they'd pretty much have to accept it, I guess. As Dave talks on about his plans to be a student missionary after his first year in college, and how he'd like to work with the Red Cross or ADRA or something after that, I have this picture in my head of me and Dave, dressed in these khaki fatigue-type shorts and shirts, feeding these poor starving children in a refugee camp somewhere in Africa or something. Suddenly I hear the sound of planes overhead and Dave grabs my hand— *Alex! The enemy planes are coming! Run for cover . . .*

"Alex?" Dave says.

I come out of my daydream to find I'm back on the beach, no refugees, no enemy planes, just Dave and me. "Sorry," I say. "I was just thinking about— what you were talking about. It would be an exciting life."

"Well, maybe we'll both do it someday," he says with a grin.

As we paddle back to camp in the canoe, I can't forget the daydream. My one big problem about being a Christian was that I always thought non-Christians had more exciting lives. I mean, I have a lot of fun with my Christian friends, but you couldn't call it *excitement*. But kids who are always breaking the rules seem to be always having some big thrill. Like Mike and the car accident. You've got to admit it was exciting. But what a sick kind of excitement—sitting around wasting time, drinking and fighting, then driving like an idiot and getting into a wreck and maybe killing someone. Wow. What a thrill. But I never realized until Dave started talking like this that being a Christian, helping other people, could be so much *more* exciting. I think I'd like an exciting life.

"I'm going to go on the Action trip again too," I tell him. "If I can possibly raise the money."

In no time the weekend is over and we're headed home. It's not easy to say goodbye to Dave, and the only thing that makes it possible is that he keeps assuring me we can work it out for me to visit him.

I catch a ride home with Liesl and her parents. Liesl's all teary-eyed because she made a lot of friends at camp this summer who were college students and now she won't see them all year. And I'd have to admit, if I were totally honest, that there's a big lump in my throat as well when I think about saying goodbye to Dave.

When the Schmidts drop me at my parents' house several

hours later, my sister Cindy and brother Jeff are out in the front yard, and they run to meet me. I haven't seen them since school let out in June. After a minute, the front door opens and my mom comes out and gives me a big hug.

It's kind of nice to be back home, and even when Dad arrives home from his hardware store he doesn't say anything too critical to me. I mean, he doesn't exactly welcome me back with open arms, but he does say, "Did you enjoy camp, Julie?" which is better than nothing.

It's not till later that night, after I've unpacked and everything, that I mention that I have this friend, Dave Vickers, who wants me to visit him next weekend. Mom just raises her eyebrows, and Dad grunts from behind his paper. He'll let Mom do all the talking and won't cut in until it's time for him to lay down the law.

"Well, Julie," Mom says, "you know we don't like the idea of you going to visit boys . . . "

"I'd be staying with his *family*, Mom," I say patiently. I might as well be patient since it is going to be the start of a long and useless argument.

"But we don't know his family, dear. We don't know anything about them, and I just don't feel comfortable with you staying with people we don't know."

"Foolishness, anyway," Dad grunts. "This is some boyfriend of yours, I suppose, Julie?"

"Yeah, he's my friend. I guess you could say he's my boyfriend."

"Not right for a girl your age to be getting serious about anyone like that. I don't intend to let you go off with him."

"I'd be visiting him at his parents' place! And it's not *serious!*"

"Going home to meet the family—that was considered serious in my day. Don't know what it's considered now."

"You have to be careful, Julie," Mom says in her pleading voice.

This goes on for a while, as I knew it would, and eventually I just say goodnight and go upstairs. They aren't going to give in so there's no point starting a fight. But the next night Dave phones long distance for me.

"So, do you think you'll be able to come down on the weekend?" he asks eagerly. It's so great just to hear his voice again.

"Um, no—not much chance of it, I'm afraid." I look across the kitchen at Mom. Dad is out, but she's hanging onto every word.

"Oh no! Your parents won't let you come?"

"Well, no."

A pause. I figure Dave is smart enough to catch on that there's someone in the room and that I can't talk all that freely. Then he says, "Alex, do you think it would help if my mom talked to your mom. She could let her know it's OK and everything."

"It's worth a try, I guess. Is she there now?"

Mom doesn't seem too anxious to get on the phone with Dave's mother, but when I pass her the phone she puts on her polite smiley voice and starts trying to explain her point of view—how she doesn't like her daughter going to stay with strangers for the weekend and thinks 16 is a little young to be dating seriously. But Dave's mom keeps her on the line talking and after a few minutes her tone of voice changes. "Is this—not Leona *Matthews?*" she says. "The one who—oh, my, Leona, I'd lost track of you completely!"

A flicker of hope crosses my mind. Obviously my mom and Dave's mom know each other. Which could make things better for him and me.

Except, of course, that we'll never get to use the phone again. Half an hour later Mom and "Leona" are still gabbing about old times and trying to discover what happened to every single one of their friends from college. Finally she remembers me and passes the phone back to me. Dave's mom is still on the line.

"Well, Alex," she says, "it looks like you may be able to come visit us after all. We'd sure like to have you. I guess you'd like to talk to David again now."

After my mom has tied up the phone for so long, she

can't really complain about me talking to Dave, so we take advantage and spin it out into a long conversation. When I finally hang up, I say, "So, it's OK, Mom? I can go?"

Mom is still smiling over her conversation with Dave's mother. "I can't believe he's Leona Matthews' boy. Well, I didn't know her married name, of course, that's why I didn't recognize it. But, my—it's been years."

"So, can I go stay with them?"

"Oh, I don't see why not. We'll have to ask your dad, though."

I don't bother saying things like *He's not my dad!* anymore. That was in my bratty phase. But I do have a real sinking feeling when I hear her words.

With good reason, it turns out. When Dad arrives home and hears the story, he's not one bit impressed that Dave's mom is Mom's old college friend Leona Matthews.

"So?" he says when Mom finishes talking. "That's all well and good, but I don't see that it changes anything. I still don't want Julie going down there."

Mom looks crushed. "Well, I thought—I just thought, since Leona's an old friend of mine, it would be nice for Julie to go there. We'd know she was in good hands."

"I don't care if it's your own twin sister she's going to visit, I don't want her staying with some boyfriend and getting ideas!" Dad says, raising his voice and getting red in the face. He used to do this every time he got mad about something but since his heart attack Mom's always trying to keep him calm and not get worked up. Which usually means everyone else has to give in sooner than they normally would. I know this is what she's going to do now—cave in so as not to upset Dad.

But Mom surprises me. She looks determined, not like her usual quiet at-home self but like her teacher self, the way she was when she taught me in elementary school, very strong and sure of herself.

"I'm sorry, Ed," she says, "but I've made up my mind. If Julie is friends with Leona Matthews' boy, then I'd be glad to have her visit their family. I was thinking of driving her down myself on Thursday so I'd have a little time to visit with Leona. I want Julie to go, and I want to take her there myself," she repeats quietly but firmly. I look at Dad, waiting for the explosion.

But there isn't one. He just shakes his head and says, "Well, you'll be doing it against my advice, I can tell you that. You'll see, someday . . ." and he walks out of the room, muttering under his breath. Mom looks at me.

"Thanks," I say.

"He's just over-protective, honey; you know that. He won't mind too much, I don't think."

I can't believe he just gave up like that instead of putting his foot down and saying no. Maybe because Mom finally put *her* foot down. I've been waiting a long time for her to stand up for me in an argument with Dad. But maybe it's even more important if she's learning to stand up for *herself*. Since Dad's heart attack in the spring, a lot of things have changed around here. Last spring I would never have gone across the room and given my mom a big hug. But that's exactly what I do now.

And, sure enough, on Thursday she does drive me to Dave's place, even though she normally hates long drives, and by that time Dad's not even complaining anymore. Mom visits all day Thursday and heads back in the late afternoon, and I stay over the weekend.

It's a great weekend. Dave and I do all kinds of things with his family—play baseball, go hiking, make cookies, watch old home videos on Saturday night. His parents are really nice to me and his younger brother and sister are kind of cute. The only bad part about it is that it really doesn't look like Dave's going to be able to come back to PVA with me next week.

"We'd love to send him," Mrs. Vickers says to me Sunday afternoon when I'm alone in the backyard with her for a few minutes. "But with two younger kids in church school and two older ones in college, we really can't afford academy for Dave—especially since we want to be able to send him to college too someday. I know academy would be a wonderful opportunity for him, but unless there's some kind of miracle in the way of financial aid, I don't see it happening."

On Monday afternoon, before Mom picks me up, Dave and I take a long walk together.

"I really hoped we could be together at school this year," he says. He stares at the ground, kicking dirt with his toe, and the way he looks is exactly the way I feel.

"I know," is all I can say. "But Dave, I had a really great weekend down here. And we can visit each other again sometime."

He just nods. Then he blurts out, "But you know, Alex, long-distance relationships don't work out all that great. You'll meet someone else at PVA you want to go out with, and it doesn't make sense to be tied down to someone who's miles away . . ."

"I don't really see that happening," I say around the sudden lump in my throat. "But let's cross that bridge when we come to it, OK? We're still the best of friends, and we always will be."

Dave's already holding my hand, but he squeezes it even tighter. "And someday we'll go work in a refugee camp together."

"You betcha."

He stops walking then, and pulls me close for a long kiss—one that's loving and sweet but sad at the same time because neither of us knows how long it will be before we're together again like this.

But in spite of Dave not being there, I'm excited about going back to school to see all my friends. I return home Monday night and spend the next couple of days packing, and then Dad and Mom drive me up to PVA.

Just as when I arrived last year, my parents give me lots of lectures about being a good girl and staying out of trouble. It doesn't bother me as much as it used to, though, because I've sort of made my own decisions about what kind of crowd I want to hang out with and what kind of things I want to do. Not because my parents have told me, but because *I* want to.

109

I'm rooming with Dana Rowley again, and when I get to the room she's already there, along with Heather and Stacey, who are in the room next to us, and Lacey and her roommate, Jennifer. Everyone's catching up on summer news and gossip.

"Oh, and don't forget to ask all about Alex's big summer romance," Heather announces when I've said hi to everyone. And so I have to tell all the girls about Dave, and show the pictures I've got of him, and stick his picture up over my desk. Everyone says he's really cute and that it's too bad he can't come to PVA this year.

Later in the evening I drop by Jackie and Shantelle's room to see if they have any news about Tammy. There's nothing new—she's doing better, but she's still up in Wilcox with her parents. And Mike, of course, couldn't come back to PVA even if he wanted to this year.

"That's OK by me," I tell Jackie. "I can't say I'm going to miss him."

"Lots of girls will," Jackie says.

Finally, Walt drops by the dorm to see me and tell me all about *his* summer. As we're sitting on the front steps of the dorm and I'm bringing him up to date on everything, who should walk by but two teachers—Mr. Edwards and Mr. Marsh. They pause to say hi.

"Of course, we're only saying hi to Walt," Mr. Marsh explains, "because we've seen more than enough of you, Miss Alex Best, all summer long."

"Oh, you think you have it bad? After seeing you driving the speedboat every day all summer, now I have to see you up front in my English class!" I laugh. "Oh, by the way," I add, "I never got a chance to tell you because you had to leave camp early, but I just want to thank you for giving me some of the *worst* advice of my life!"

Mr. Marsh wrinkles his brow. "I gave you advice?" Mr. Edwards and Walt stop talking to listen.

"Yeah. Remember we were talking one time and you told me sometimes a person should just go back and find out what would have happened with someone they used to like—just to see if it would work out, so they wouldn't always be wondering? That's what I came back here that weekend to see—a certain male person, and got into that stupid car accident!"

Mr. Marsh looks totally blank, but Mr. Edwards bursts out laughing and slaps him on the shoulder. "That's what you get for talking about your private life to students, Marsh!" he says. "She thought you were giving *her* advice, instead of taking it yourself."

"Huh?" I ask. Now it's my turn to look puzzled.

Mr. Edwards explains, "Your English teacher here is too shy to tell you this himself, but he's managed to rekindle the flame of an old romance this summer. He went down to visit his old college girlfriend—you remember, Miss Nichol from Green Mountain Academy?—and I guess his visit worked out a little better than yours!"

"Miss Nichol?" I reply. "Mrs. Krause's friend? You mean—*she* was the one—you weren't giving me advice at all, were you? You were making up your *own* mind about what to do!"

"This is all getting *much* too personal. I'll see both of *you* in English class on Monday," he says, walking away with a grin.

"And don't be surprised if you hear wedding bells sometime in the future," Mr. Edwards calls over his shoulder as they leave.

"Well!" I say when they're gone. "Guess it's been a very romantic summer for some people. Mr. Marsh is back with his old girlfriend, it looks like Stacey and Bruce are getting back together, and there's—"

"Me and Vicky," Walt says happily, because they're still together apparently.

"That's right."

"And you and Dave."

"Yeah. Me and Dave. Only I might never—"

"Hey, Alex!" A familiar voice rings out across campus. Over in the parking lot by the guys' dorm, a tall blond guy is getting suitcases out of the trunk of a car. I stand up to look. It can't be—but yes. It is.

"It's Dave!" I squeal as I jump up and run over to the parking lot. He's already running toward me. After all, I think, his mom said it would take a miracle for him to come here. And I've already found out God's good at miracles. I think this particular miracle is going to make my junior year just about perfect.